Jared was out of his comfort zone.

He was used to women who wore comfortable shirts tucked into jeans. Maggie Tate wore enough pink to be a flamingo. She didn't look old enough to be a parent, let alone one who gave advice when the going got tough.

"The most important things I can tell you are don't be afraid to ask for help, take all the advice that is offered and also be willing to sacrifice to get it."

"Sacrifice?"

"Time mostly. You asked me for advice," Maggie reminded him. "Funny, but it all goes back to something we talked about the first time we met. Here's the truth. When dealing with Caleb, patience isn't a virtue—it's your only barrier between sanity and chaos."

Great, Jared thought, because if he remembered correctly, she had told him on that first meeting that patience was seldom found in a woman and never in a man.

Books by Pamela Tracy

Love Inspired

Daddy for Keeps
Once Upon a Cowboy
Once Upon a Christmas

Love Inspired Suspense

Pursuit of Justice
The Price of Redemption
Broken Lullaby
Fugitive Family
Clandestine Cover-Up

PAMELA TRACY

is an award-winning author who lives with her husband (he claims to be the inspiration for most of her heroes) and son (he claims to be the interference for most of her writing time). She started writing at a very young age—a series of romances, all with David Cassidy as the hero. Sometimes Bobby Sherman would interfere. Then, while earning a BA in journalism at Texas Tech University in Lubbock, Texas, she picked up the pen again. (This time it was an electric typewriter on which she wrote a very bad science-fiction novel.)

First published in 1999, Pamela is a winner of the American Christian Fiction Writer's Book of the Year award and has been a RITA® Award finalist. Readers can write to her at www.pamelakayetracy.com or c/o Love Inspired Books, 233 Broadway, Suite 1001, New York, NY 01279. You can find out more about Pamela by visiting her blog, Craftie Ladies of Suspense, at www.ladiesofsuspense.blogspot.com.

Once Upon a Christmas

Pamela Tracy

Love Inspired

Recycling programs
for this product may
not exist in your area.

™ LOVE INSPIRED BOOKS

ISBN-13: 978-0-373-87772-0

ONCE UPON A CHRISTMAS

www.LoveInspiredBooks.com

Printed in U.S.A.

For the Lord searches every heart
and understands every motive behind the thoughts.
—*1 Chronicles* 28:9

To my vintage shopping buddies
and fellow English teachers—Marianne Botos,
Lyn McClelland and Stacey Rannik—
you guys keep me stylish and sane. Thanks so much!

Chapter One

"I didn't hit her." Small arms folded across his chest, bottom lip at a salute, five-year-old Caleb McCreedy looked ready for battle.

Only three months into his kindergarten year and he'd managed what his two older brothers hadn't.

A trip to the principal's office.

"My lunch box hit her," Caleb finished. He made a face and paused as if in deep thought.

John Deere baseball cap in hand, Jared McCreedy shifted uncomfortably on one of the hard brown chairs in the too small office and frowned. His youngest son was no stranger to battle. He had the example of two older brothers. They, however, knew better than to bring it to school.

Mrs. Ann Tyson, principal of Roanoke Elementary for all of three months, turned to Jared as if expecting him to do something besides sit and listen as the story unfolded. Although his memories of being in trouble a time or two should have helped him speak up, they hadn't.

All he could do was frown.

"On purpose!" This outburst came from Cassidy Tate, a loud, little girl with wild brown curls.

The principal cleared her throat, not because she needed

to, Jared could tell, but to let Cassidy know she'd been out of line. Then Mrs. Tyson glanced at the referral in her hand.

Jared took the time to study Cassidy. He'd heard about her many, many times from his middle son who sat behind her in a second-grade classroom.

Cassidy tore my paper.

Cassidy pulled the head off my LEGO and now I can't find it. Never mind that Matt wasn't allowed to take LEGOs to school.

Cassidy keeps following me.

"I like her," Caleb informed the family every time Matt shared a "Cassidy" story. With Caleb, it was a love/hate relationship. Caleb loved her when he wasn't throwing lunch boxes at her, and Matt, although he wasn't allowed to hate, avoided her at all costs.

Cassidy's mother, Maggie Tate, sat on the brown chair right next to Jared, but she didn't look uncomfortable. At one time or another she must have spent time in a principal's office, too, because she seemed to know exactly what to do, how to sit and what questions to ask. She looked in control, something he wanted very much to feel at the moment.

Since his wife's death, Jared had tried for control but realized that his idea of being in control didn't mesh with the chaos of his three sons, each with varying needs and each missing their mother.

He wished Mandy were here.

When the principal finally set down the referral, Maggie was ready. "Are you sure it was on purpose?" She didn't raise her voice, change her expression, or so much as clench a fist.

"I'm sure." Cassidy glared at Caleb who was trying hard not to wriggle in a couch designed for much bigger people.

That couch hadn't been here the first time Jared had visited this office. He'd been five years old and had taken something that hadn't belonged to him. He no longer remembered what.

The next time he'd stood before the same principal's door, it was because the principal, Billy Staples, wanted permission to take something from Jared.

Jared remembered what. As oldest son, albeit in junior high, he'd willingly given his permission for his mother and Billy to marry.

Mrs. Tyson leaned forward, and Jared could see her fighting back a smile even as she said, "He did throw the lunch box up in the air on purpose. Three times. Along with five other little boys. The lunch aide asked them to stop. Two did. The aide was on her way over to intervene, yet again, when Caleb's lunch box hit Cassidy in the face."

"I wasn't aiming for her face," Caleb insisted, his voice breaking. "We were trying to see if—since our lunch boxes had peanut butter on them—they would stick to the roof if we threw them hard enough."

"Ceiling," Cassidy corrected.

Beside him, Maggie made a low-pitched, strangled sound. If Jared hadn't been sitting so close to her, he wouldn't have noticed. She was a master at keeping calm.

"But the fact that you might hit someone is exactly why the aide asked you to stop," the principal said patiently.

"And you didn't listen," Jared added, finally getting his voice.

"But—"

"No buts."

"If you'd packed me leftover turkey from Thanksgiving, like I wanted," Caleb accused, "this wouldn't have happened. Turkey doesn't stick."

"Caleb!"

Caleb had the good sense to stop talking.

Cassidy looked from Caleb to Jared before saying, "See, Mama, I told you it wasn't me."

Now that Jared looked again, the woman in question didn't look old enough to be so in control of the situation, let alone a mama, or a business owner. Yet, she was all three. This past summer, Joel, Jared's younger brother, had done some work on her vintage clothing shop. Because Joel's fiancée wanted a vintage wedding, Joel had spent a lot of time talking about vintage clothes and about the shopkeeper. His description hadn't done Maggie Tate justice.

Her deep brown hair fell in a blunt cut that was shorter than he liked and barely reached her shoulders. When she'd walked into the principal's office, five minutes late and looking non-repentant, he'd noted the short gray-and-red dress that gave him a chance to admire a nice pair of legs encased in some sort of black tights. Black clunky shoes with ridiculous heels finished the outfit.

City girl.

She'd probably been chatting up a customer in her store when she'd gotten the call from the school. He'd been in the field wrapping up corn harvest.

She smelled of some sort of jasmine perfume; he smelled of sweat.

"…not the first time for either of them," Mrs. Tyson was saying.

"What?" Jared straightened up. He'd missed the first half of the sentence.

Again came the half smile and Jared knew the principal was enjoying this. Maybe because Jared's stepfather had been principal of Roanoke Elementary for thirty years and some parents still went to him first, only to be redirected back to Mrs. Tyson. Maybe because Mrs. Tyson had heard about the McCreedy boys, and their escapades, even though more than a decade had passed since they'd been students here. Maybe because Mrs. Tyson knew the color in Jared's cheeks wasn't because Caleb was in trouble but because it had been far too long since he had admired a pair of legs.

"I was talking about throwing lunch boxes. This is not the first time for either of them."

Maggie looked at Cassidy. "Were you throwing lunch boxes, too?"

"Not today."

"But some other day?" Maggie insisted. "Did you hit Caleb with a lunch box some other day?"

Cassidy's lips went together. The answer was in her expression. Yes.

The principal's brows went together. Clearly, this was the first she'd heard of it.

"Why did you tattle," Maggie asked, "if you've done the same thing to him?"

Caleb and Cassidy exchanged a look, no longer adversaries, now conspirators.

"She didn't tattle," Mrs. Tyson said. "The aide did and the aide had plenty to say. Seems that while Caleb was removed from the lunchroom and escorted to his teacher, Cassidy hid his lunch box and doesn't seem to remember where."

Jared closed his eyes. Caleb's teacher was soon to be Jared's sister-in-law.

"We'll take care of this at home," he said firmly as he stood, giving Caleb a look that said *we're going.* "I promise you that."

"We'll find the lunch box," Maggie quickly offered. "Or—" she shot Cassidy a glance that could only mean trouble "—we'll buy him a new one from *your* allowance."

Cassidy's mouth opened to an exaggerated *O*. That quickly, Caleb was back to adversary.

"If he threw the lunch box at her, she's not buying him a new one," Jared argued.

"People." One word, that's all it took when it was an elementary school principal.

Ten minutes later, Jared stood outside the principal's office door tightly holding Caleb's hand. Maggie and her daughter were still inside.

"This is my baddest day." Caleb didn't even try to fight

the tears. Of Jared's three boys, he was the one who cried freely, whined often and ran full tilt from the time he got out of bed until he fell back into it. He argued the most, too. But, Caleb was also the one who still climbed on Jared's lap, laughed until tears came to his eyes and who knew the name of each and every animal on the farm.

If they didn't have a name, Caleb gave them one.

"I doubt that," Jared said calmly. "We'll talk later. Now, don't start whining."

"I can't help it. I really want my lunch box. It's my favorite."

Jared pictured the lunch boxes sitting on the kitchen counter. Grandpa Billy packed them every morning. Ryan's was a plain blue. Nine-year-olds no longer needed action figures or at least his didn't. Matt's was Star Wars. Caleb's was Spider-Man.

"We should go buy a new one," Caleb suggested. "There's a really cool one—"

"No, we should go to the cafeteria and see if the lunch ladies found it."

Caleb followed, feet dragging. "I don't want to go there."

Of course he didn't. The principal had just assigned him a full week of wiping down tables instead of going to recess. Jared intended to do the same at home along with no television for a week.

The cafeteria hadn't changed all that much since Jared's years. There were still rows of tables with benches that could be levered up to make mopping easier. Large gray trash baskets were in the four corners. Right now, decorations of snowflakes and wrapped presents were taped to the walls. Snowmen and Santas shared messages of "Don't Forget our Winter Program."

No way could Jared forget. He'd recently been put in charge of props. In just a few weeks, Caleb would be dressed like an elf and singing with his class. Ryan actually had the part of Santa. Matt would pretend to have a stomachache the night of the program. According to the note sent by Matt's teacher, he had the role of delivering presents to people in the audience.

Smart teacher.

"You start in here," Jared ordered. "I'll go in the kitchen."

A few minutes later, Maggie Tate joined them in the search. She poked her head in the kitchen door. "I'm so sorry. She'll be wiping down lunch tables with him."

Jared almost bumped his head as he looked up from the cabinet he'd been going through. "That's okay."

She nodded and then went into the cafeteria, presumably to search.

Jared was on his fifth cabinet when he heard the giggles.

He followed the noise to the cafeteria and stopped. In the middle of the lunchroom tables stood Maggie and the two children, all of them looking at the ceiling. In her hand, she held Caleb's lunch box. Jared could see the peanut butter smeared all over it.

Finally, Maggie hunched down and shook her head. "Caleb, it would take a lot more peanut butter to make it stick."

"I wondered about that," Caleb admitted.

"I can go find some peanut butter," Cassidy offered.

Maggie simply shook her head again, smiled at Jared and sashayed past him into the kitchen where she washed the offending lunch box before handing it to Jared.

For a brief moment he'd been worried she'd gone looking for peanut butter.

Maggie helped Cassidy into her coat and out the front door of Roanoke Elementary. Together they walked the mere block to Maggie's shop Hand Me Ups.

Well, Maggie walked; Cassidy did more of a sideways hop with a scoot and jiggle follow-up.

"I don't think it's fair that I got in so much trouble," Cassidy said after a moment. "I didn't throw my lunch box at him, and we found the lunch box right where I hid it. And I only hid it so he wouldn't throw it at me again."

"But you didn't tell people where you hid the lunch box when they asked. That was wrong."

Cassidy contemplated, for all of thirty seconds. "But, if I gave it back, he might have thrown it at me again."

"Once adults were involved, that wasn't likely. You were wasting our time. I might have missed a customer at the shop. And I'm sure Caleb's dad had work to do. Plus, even you admitted he didn't exactly 'throw' it at you."

"Oh, yeah."

"And, what if the lunch box was gone when we went back to get it?" Maggie asked.

"He could have one of mine."

Cassidy had two, both pink and both secondhand, one with Dora on it and the other with Cinderella. Cassidy's greatest wish was to get rid of both of them in order to buy a new one with a pony on it. Maggie doubted Caleb would be inclined to accept either.

"No, if the lunch box disappeared, we'd be getting him a new one, with your piggy bank money."

"But I have to use that money to buy presents!" Cassidy's scoot and jiggle stopped for all of a moment. Then, she was on to a new subject: one where her piggy bank wasn't in danger and there were other problems to solve. "Am I pretty?"

"Getting prettier every day."

"Today, Lisa Totwell said that she was the prettiest girl in class and that I was second."

"Well," Maggie said carefully, "do you want to be the prettiest, or is it okay if Lisa is?"

"It's okay if she is. She's my best friend, you know. Cuz we're both the new students in second grade this year. Everyone else has been here forever."

Yesterday, Brittney Callahan had been Cassidy's best friend. Before that, it was Sarah, a girl Maggie had yet to put a last name or a face to.

Didn't matter. Maggie was thrilled at how quickly Cassidy was fitting in—maybe fitting in a little too well. Coming to Roanoke, Iowa, was the right choice. For both of them.

"Cassidy, you know that Caleb is only in kindergarten, right?"

"Yep."

"Maybe you need to play with the kids in your own class."

Cassidy stopped so quickly, she nearly stumbled to the ground. "No way, Mom. Caleb is my friend, and he's fun. Plus, he's Matt's brother."

Matt McCreedy was the subject of many a conversation. He was the only one in Cassidy's second grade who hadn't been given best-friend status, and Maggie suspected Cassidy might be going through her first crush.

Now that Maggie had met Matt's dad, she figured he and Matt were cut from the same cloth—rugged, sturdy denim. Caleb seemed to be cut from a different sort of cloth.

Which meant that Mr. Jared McCreedy didn't understand his youngest son's creative personality.

"We'll talk about it later." Maggie didn't want to dwell on the plight of the misunderstood child.

She'd been one—an army brat with an errant mother and a father who was used to giving orders and having them followed with a "Yes, sir. Right away, sir." Her dad was a man who tried hard, but one who definitely didn't understand girls.

"Mom, you've got that look on your face again," Cassidy complained. "Did I do something?"

"Yes, you did something. You got sent to the principal's office for the second time, and I had to leave work to come deal with it. After taking most of last week off, I really needed to spend time in the shop."

Cassidy suddenly was very involved in staring at a crack in the sidewalk.

Maggie wasn't deterred. "School's only been in session three months. Next week is December and if you don't..." Her words tapered off as a black truck drove by. Actually, she was glad for the interruption. She'd been about to bring up consequences, such as not attending Christmas activity at the church this Friday night or even the school's winter play and the possibility of Cassidy not appearing in it.

Don't threaten unless you mean it.

"Look, Mom!"

Jared McCreedy sat tall and oh-so-serious-looking behind the wheel of the Ford diesel truck. His three sons, the oldest in the front, two more in the back, all looked at Maggie and Cassidy. Caleb waved. Except for Matt, none of the boys appeared as serious as their father.

Cassidy frowned. "They have a dog. His name is Captain Rex."

Something Cassidy asked for quite often, usually after figuring out that there was no way her mother would even listen when asked for a horse or a baby brother.

"Yes, they have a dog."

Cassidy's letter to Santa—not mailed because it wasn't finished—had a dog in it, second on the list, right after a pair of red boots. Cassidy wouldn't be getting a dog. The McCreedys had something Maggie and Cassidy did not: *a house and yard*. Maggie thought of two more things the Mc-Creedys had: *horses and baby brothers*.

And family. They had plenty of family. They hadn't had to fly to New York to celebrate Thanksgiving with her disapproving mother-in-law—the only relative who cared even to invite them.

The McCreedys, Maggie knew, had roots that ran deep in Roanoke, Iowa. She hadn't seen Solitaire Farm, their place, but she'd heard about it and could picture what it looked like.

Big white house with a huge porch, complete with a swing and a rocker or two. Long driveway, winding its way to the front door, cars parked, meaning a large family. A barn. Lots of green, green grass to run across and trees to climb. Room to breathe. Plenty of animals, especially horses and, of course, acres of corn and soybeans.

Except for the corn, soybeans and animals bigger than a dog, what Maggie imagined was pretty much a portrait of one of her goals: a real home for Cassidy.

Too bad this farm was owned by a man who reminded her of her late husband, Dan, thinking of his duty above all else. Because, if Jared McCreedy had been a different kind of man—softer, more jubilant and easygoing—maybe Maggie would have engaged in a little flirting.

What would it have hurt?

It had been a year.

Not a chance. Jared even looked like Maggie's late husband: tall, thick dark brown hair, and almost black piercing eyes. Both men were capable of walking into a room and suddenly making the room seem small. There were a few differences. Dan wore fatigues while Jared wore jeans and a flannel shirt. Dan had to wear his hair at a precision cut while Jared's was long enough to cover his ears. Dan was always clean-shaven. Jared had a five-o'clock shadow that made Maggie think about how good whiskers felt during a kiss.

Whoa.

Been there, done that, not a chance Maggie wanted to deal with a man so intent on being in control that he didn't know how to have fun.

Or appreciate the concept of getting a lunch box to stick to the ceiling with the help of a little peanut butter. Maggie smiled when she pictured the abject horror on Jared's face when she spotted the sticky lunch box. No, Jared McCreedy was not her ideal man. No sense of thinking about him at all.

Chapter Two

It had been a tough week thanks to Monday's phone call from the principal. And now once again, thanks to a Friday phone call from Caleb's teacher, Jared was standing in the hallway of Roanoke Elementary.

He checked his watch. He had at least a dozen things to do today, starting with figuring out—since he was here—what props were needed for the school's Christmas program. The father who had been in charge was now working extra hours and Beth, the woman he was about to see, had asked Joel, her fiancé and Jared's brother, to help.

Joel had a rodeo, so right now, Jared was it.

But that had nothing to do with his visit today. No, Beth had something to say about Caleb, his youngest, who was responsible for Jared standing in the school's hallway at four in the afternoon on a working day.

Through a window in the door, he could see Beth sitting at a small table. Someone else's mom had her back to the door. So, maybe Caleb wasn't the only one in trouble. Both women seemed overly fascinated by some paperwork spread out on the small table.

He didn't intend to let any more time pass doing nothing. He needed to gather his boys, find the teacher in charge of the program, talk shop and head home. There was still an hour or two of Iowa daylight, and he had things to do and was already behind. He opened the classroom door and stepped in.

"Jared." Beth Armstrong—Miss Armstrong to his son, Beth to him—twisted in her seat, looking surprised.

Funny, she'd called his cell phone and left a message requesting this meeting.

Then she glanced at the large clock just over her desk. "Is it that time already?"

"That time and then some," Jared said, finally figuring out who was sitting with Beth. Hmm, she didn't have a child in Beth's class. Had something else happened between Caleb and Cassidy?

His future sister-in-law didn't even blink, just nonchalantly walked over to where Jared stood. "Sorry, I was looking at pictures of wedding dresses and time got away from me. You know Maggie, right?"

"Away from us," Maggie Tate agreed as she closed magazines and reached for some loose pictures, "and, yes, we've met."

When Jared didn't respond, didn't say that keeping him waiting was okay, Beth grinned. She was getting entirely too good at teasing him. He could blame the fact that she was about to become his sister-in-law, but truth was, he'd known her most of his life. This time, she simply told him something he already knew. "Patience is a virtue."

"Whoever coined that phrase wasn't a single father of three with a farm to run," Jared retorted.

"And I didn't realize that you were standing outside waiting for Beth." Maggie finished loading the papers into a canvas bag and made her way to the door. Jared couldn't help but think her small frame looked right at home in the five-year-old wonderland of kindergarten.

His mouth went dry, and the annoyance he felt at being kept waiting almost vanished.

Almost.

Then, the young woman, her eyes twinkling, spoke again. "Patience is a virtue, have it if you can. Seldom found in a woman. Never in a man."

Beth clapped her hands, clearly pleased that someone else shared the same opinion.

All Jared could think was, *great, another female with a proverb.* The only sayings he knew by heart were the ones his father said, and they were more advice than quips. Jared's personal favorite: always plow around a stump.

He doubted the women would appreciate his contribution.

"Maggie's helping me find my wedding dress," Beth said.

"You're a wedding planner, too?" Jared asked, forcing his gaze from Maggie's deep green eyes. He had no time for a pretty face. And he was more than annoyed.

"Wedding planner?" Beth looked confused.

"I'm willing to add that to my list of occupations," Maggie said. "But, at the moment, no. I'm just a shop owner and seamstress trying to keep a customer happy."

Her shop, Jared knew, was all about vintage clothing, which explained the red velvet skirt. Who wore red velvet? Maybe Santa. Jared suppressed the smile that threatened to emerge. This woman was as alien to his world as, well, as an alien. Her skirt, tight at the knees, reminded him of one Marilyn Monroe had worn in an old movie he'd watched. She'd topped it with a simple white shirt and wide black belt. It was colder today than it had been on Monday. Maybe that's why she had on a tiny, red sweater.

She'd freeze going out to the car.

Square-toed boots completed the outfit and kept Jared from admiring her legs the way he'd just admired her figure.

Good.

Frilly city girls made no sense to him.

Plus, she looked like she was ready to assist Santa or something.

"When I finished talking with my daughter's teacher," Maggie explained, "I checked to see if Beth happened to be alone. I'd brought some samples for her to look at." Her voice was louder than Beth's, stronger, and with an accent he couldn't quite place, but definitely not Midwestern.

"I need to fetch Cassidy before she thinks I've forgotten her." Maggie carefully slid by Jared, grabbed a coat from on top of a student's desk and hurried toward the exit. "I'll get going and let you have your time."

"See if you can find me something like the first one we looked at," Beth called.

Jared didn't say anything, just held open the door so Maggie could exit gracefully.

"I really am sorry," Beth said. "Time got away from me. And I do need to talk with you."

Jared folded himself into the small orange chair Maggie'd just vacated. A fragrance that didn't belong to five-year-olds or their teacher lingered—that jasmine smell again. He waited while Beth went to her desk and rummaged through a stack of papers.

Jared did his best not to hurry her. Unfortunately, the seconds ticked on and Jared started imagining all the suggestions she had for him. She probably wanted him to work with Caleb more. Jared got that, and would love suggestions, especially when it came to time management and incentives.

He stared at a bulletin board with a group of Christmas trees, stickers acting as ornaments, all bearing the names of Caleb's classmates.

Caleb's ornament read *C-A-B*. The *B* looked ready to fall down. Jared's youngest son hadn't bothered with the *L* or the *E*.

"Caleb behaving? I've asked him every day since Monday. He claims his light's been green."

Jared understood the traffic light system. Green meant Go, everything good. Yellow meant Pause, we need to think about this day and perhaps discuss how it could have been a bit better. Red meant no television, or no video games, or no LEGO bricks, depending on which kid decided not to obey the rules.

Beth didn't answer, but finally found whatever she was looking for and came to sit down with Jared. She laid a few papers in front of him. "Caleb is trying very hard to behave but he complains a lot about his stomach hurting. He asks to go to the bathroom often."

"He does that at home, too," Jared admitted.

"Behavior is not why I called."

She took a breath, and suddenly Jared got worried.

"It's still very early," Beth said softly, "and maybe if I hadn't been around since Caleb was born, I'd wait. But, the music and PE teacher have both come to me with concerns, also. Jared, it's not that he's misbehaving, but he's having trouble focusing, not just your typical trouble, either. Caleb can't wait his turn, he bursts out with answers and he's unable to sit long enough to complete a single paper."

For a moment, Jared had trouble wrapping his mind around what Beth was saying. Yes, of his three boys, Caleb was the most energetic. Okay, downright wild at times. Jared saw that and somewhat blamed himself. After his wife, Mandy, had died four years ago, Jared had buried himself in the farm. For the first year, he'd walked around in a black fog. The three years that followed were a transitional period. He should have been paying more attention to Caleb.

But Caleb was still very young, only five.

"I think you need to schedule an appointment with your family doctor, see what he thinks. Honestly, Jared," Beth continued, "I'm hoping it's just immaturity, but if it's not, I want to get help now so that first grade and beyond are easier. We might need to think about having some testing done and maybe seeing a developmental specialist."

"Developmental specialist?" Jared's tongue felt twice its

normal size. Judging by his inability to say more than one or two words, he felt more like an observer to this conference than a participant. He shook his head and wished—like he wished almost every day—that Mandy were here instead of him, making these decisions when it came to this part of parenthood. Mandy always seemed to know what to do.

"Jared?" Beth said.

He looked at her, desperately trying to think of a response. "I think Caleb is fine," he finally said. "He can count to a hundred. He's been able to add and subtract single digits since he was three. You've trained my brother well. He's been helping all the boys with math while they work at Solitaire's Market."

"I know, Jared," she said softly. "Caleb likes numbers."

He scooted back the chair and stood. "Do you have anything else you need to tell me?"

She looked at him, and he saw in her eyes so many shared memories. She'd been his late wife's best friend and truly loved his sons.

"Caleb's a charmer, but you already knew that."

Jared nodded, wanting more than anything to get out of this room where everything was in miniature and the dominant smell was no longer jasmine but crayons, glue and children. He needed to get home, back in the field, where he could wrestle his oversize tractor and surround himself with the land, McCreedy land, and the rich smell of dirt that would not forsake.

Beth stood and held out yet another piece of paper, this time not one with Caleb's scribbles. "It's the developmental specialist the school recommends, just in case."

"I didn't even know the town was big enough to have a developmental specialist."

"It's not big enough," Beth said. "You'll have to go to Des Moines."

"That's over an hour."

And still Beth held out the paper. He took it because he'd neither the time nor the inclination to argue. He went into Des Moines maybe once every two or three months. "I'll think about it," he finally said.

"You know," Beth said thoughtfully, "you might want to talk to Maggie. She's a friend and she's told me to give her name to any parent needing help. Her daughter Cassidy's just two years older than Caleb and has problems with focus, too. She's already walking the path you're about to travel."

"I work best alone," Jared said.

As he closed the door behind him, he heard her utter one word.

"Liar."

Maggie pushed her chair away from the kitchen table and rested her elbows on the windowsill. She could feel the cold coming through the pane but she didn't care, at least not enough to move. Tiny slivers of aged gold paint flecked onto the sleeves of her pink sweater. She did care a bit about the moisture gathering in the center of the pane. It meant she needed to replace the window.

One more thing on her list.

Just a month ago, Roanoke, Iowa, boasted a distant sea of green, orange, red and yellow leaves that Maggie could see from her second-story window. The sight of so many trees, some stretching over residential streets, never failed to take her breath away.

Because the view belonged to her.

Today, the trees stretched their empty, dark limbs like waiting fingers saying, *Where's the snow? We're waiting.*

It was *her* town. Just like the trees, she intended to put down roots, grow, thrive, make a home, never leave.

Please let this be a forever kind of place.

Even now, in the predawn light, her town was waking up and starting its day. Just like she was doing.

Across the wide street was a drugstore. It had the old-timey chairs but the only thing the owner served up was Thrifty ice cream. Maggie dreamed of a soda fountain. Next to it was a hardware store that Maggie avoided because the only things she liked to fix simply needed a needle and thread. Then there was an antiques store she couldn't resist. The owner, one Henry Throxmorton, was unlocking the front door. He had a newspaper under his arm. She'd never seen him smile, but she knew his wife was sick a lot. Maybe that was why.

Just two days ago, Maggie had found in Roanoke's Rummage—an awful name for an antiques store if you asked Maggie—the pair of red cowboy boots she'd been looking for. Looking unloved and extremely dusty, they'd been on the bottom shelf of a bookcase. There was no rhyme or reason to how Henry arranged his store. But, had they been on display, maybe some other enterprising mother would have found them.

All it took to make them look almost new was a thorough cleaning with saddle soap and then applying a cream-based polish of the same color. They were already wrapped and under the Christmas tree.

On the same side was also a small real estate office. Maggie sometimes dawdled by the front where there were pictures of homes for sale. The ones with big lawns attracted her the most, but she didn't really do yard work. The ones with no backyards didn't appeal at all.

Looking at the photos also exposed a curiosity Maggie had finally acted on. Her mother had been born in Roanoke in 1967. Could one of the houses have been her childhood home? Maggie didn't have a clue. All she remembered of her mother was a woman who smoked cigarettes and cooked a lot of noodle soup.

Maggie hated noodle soup.

Life had handed Maggie's mother an itinerary that she

didn't intend to follow. It included the destinations marriage and motherhood. The only reason Maggie knew about Roanoke was her mother's birth certificate. Natalie had been seven pounds, six ounces, and twenty-one-inches long: a live birth, Caucasian. She'd been born to Mary Johnson. Either Mary had chosen not to put down a name for the father or she hadn't known who the father was.

So, some help that was. In Roanoke, Johnson was the second-most popular name, nestled between Smith and Miller.

Moving to Roanoke to find a connection to an errant mother was akin to looking for a needle in a haystack and made about as much sense. But Maggie had two choices. Stay in New York with Dan's mother or strike out on her own.

She didn't regret her choice and there was nothing wrong with living above one's place of business. It was very convenient in fact. But Cassidy needed a backyard, a place to run, a swing set, the dog she kept asking for. No, not the horse. And Maggie wanted her own bedroom.

Maybe in a few years.

Maggie shook off the daydream. This morning was a school day and tonight was a holiday party at Beth's church. Cassidy had begged to go, had already planned what to wear. Maggie had too much to do to dawdle in front of the window any longer.

After brushing off the paint—she really needed to do something about sanding and repainting—she scooted back to her computer and started to push away some of Cassidy's school papers. Why they were on Maggie's desk, she didn't know. Cassidy's stuff seemed to have a mind of its own and liked to spread to every nook and cranny of their tiny apartment.

Cassidy's letter to Santa was under a page of math homework, and it looked like her list had grown to three. Underneath the word *puppy* was added *baby brother*.

Great, another item that couldn't be purchased at a discount store. Cassidy needed to start thinking of affordable alternatives or the red boots would be it.

If only the red boots could bark and be named Fido.

While Cassidy slumbered, Maggie—sitting next to the old wall heater and thinking about turning on the oven—updated the store's records on her computer. Under her breath, she reminded herself that any small business needed four years to establish. Right now, thanks to her alteration business, she made enough to pay the bills and a few, very few, extras. Oh, it caused some late and restless nights, but with the economy the way it was, Maggie was just glad she had a way to make a living. So what if she went to the library instead of the bookstore. So what if they ate hamburgers instead of steaks.

Maggie had enough money for the essentials.

The used red cowboy boots under the tree were proof of that. She'd priced new red boots. Not this Christmas. Good thing hugs were free.

Finally, at seven, Maggie turned off the computer and headed for the kitchen to make breakfast. Cassidy still slept and Maggie wouldn't wake her until the blueberry pancakes were ready, one large circle for a face, two small ovals for ears, then banana slices for eyes, a strawberry nose and raisin teeth.

It was a tradition that Maggie knew would end all too soon as her little girl grew up. Just when Maggie picked up a spoon, the doorbell rang.

Maggie quickly glanced at the calendar on the refrigerator. Two reminders were penciled in.

The only pickup Maggie had today was Rosalind Maynard. She'd wanted Maggie to find a 1930s denim chore jacket for her husband. They were getting their photo made for their seventieth wedding anniversary. Apparently, Rosalind's husband came from a long line of farmers. His parents had also had a seventieth photo taken way back when, and George Jr. wanted to look like his dad, even down to the jacket.

It was the second notation that made Maggie frown. Yesterday, Jared McCreedy had called. He wanted to talk. She'd agreed, and she'd said any morning was good, but she hadn't planned on this *soon*.

No, not possible. This morning was too soon for it to be Jared.

She hoped.

Quickly, Maggie hurried down the stairs and skidded, barefoot, across the cold, wooden floor. Maybe she could open the door, usher in Mrs. Maynard, grab the jacket, ring up the sale, usher out the customer, and still get her kid fed and to school on time.

Only it wasn't Mrs. Maynard.

Jared McCreedy stood on the threshold, three boys by his side and cap in hand. He didn't say a word when she threw open the door. He pretty much just stared.

His son Caleb wasn't so shy. "Wow, I think you like pink."

"Hush," Jared said.

Hiding a smile, Maggie stepped back and let the entire clan in.

"Pink is a good color," Maggie said to Caleb, "which is why I'm wearing it. I call this my Jane Fonda look." Granted, leg warmers were very seventies, but she did own a vintage store, so she could get away with it.

"I like red," Caleb admitted.

An older boy shook her hand, the only McCreedy she hadn't met personally, and then sat on a chair right by the entry and whipped out some sort of handheld gaming device.

"That's Ryan," Caleb announced. "He's in fourth grade."

Matt looked around suspiciously. "Where's Cassidy?"

"Upstairs asleep."

"It's time to go to school." Matt was completely aghast.

"I was just making her breakfast when you rang the doorbell. We're fast eaters and dressers."

Matt, way too mature for a second grader, clearly had more to say on the subject, but Jared jumped in. "We don't need to be keeping you. I saw your lights on, we were running early, and I don't know what I was thinking stopping by unannounced. I'm so sorry. I can stop back by once I've dropped the boys off at school if that's okay. I got up at five and thanks to the party tonight at church, I have a whole list of things to do. That's no excuse, though. I simply forget the rest of the world can sleep in."

It had been a week since she'd last seen Jared. He still managed to have that my-time-is-too-valuable-for-this look on his handsome face, but right now there was a hint of something else, maybe humbleness.

"I get up at five, too, Monday through Friday," Maggie responded. "It's when I do the books. That way my evening belongs to Cassidy."

Jared shook his head. His dark hair, combed to the side, didn't move. He opened his mouth, but instead of addressing Maggie, he looked past her and said sternly, "Caleb, those stairs do not belong to you."

Halfway up the stairs Caleb paused indecisively, but before the little boy could make a decision, a loud thump, the sound of something breaking and then a howl came from above.

"Cassidy," Maggie breathed.

The only McCreedy who beat her to the apartment's kitchen was Caleb.

Cassidy stood in the middle of the room crying. Pancake batter splattered her pajama bottoms, the floor, the counters, the refrigerator door and even the ceiling. The bowl was in pieces.

"Now that's a mess," Matt said from behind her.

Jared's snort could have been dismay, agreement, or it

could have been him holding back laughter. Maggie couldn't see his face.

"Don't move," Maggie ordered. Quickly she stepped amid the batter and shards, lifted her howling child under her arms and carried Cassidy into the bathroom. Flipping shut the toilet lid with her foot, Maggie stood her daughter on top and asked, "Are you bleeding?"

Cassidy continued howling.

Maggie knew neither cajoling nor scolding would have any effect. So, in a matter-of-fact voice, she reasoned, "Matt, from your class, is here. Do you want him to tell your friends that you're a crybaby?"

Cassidy stopped.

"Now," Maggie went on, gently wiping the tears from Cassidy's face, "are you bleeding?"

"Yes."

"Where?"

Cassidy searched desperately for some blood.

After a moment, Maggie nudged in a patient but firm voice, "Where do you hurt?"

The fact that Cassidy had to stop and think proved what Maggie already knew. Cassidy wasn't bleeding and she wasn't hurt. She was scared and embarrassed. The best cure for that was not a bandage but a hug.

Hugs were free.

A minute later, Cassidy was in her room changing into her school clothes and Maggie was in her kitchen trying not to stare as a tall cowboy, too tall for this tiny kitchen, cleaned up pancake batter.

Chapter Three

After eating a second breakfast, because Maggie offered and it seemed polite and, okay, Jared needed something to do with his hands, he ushered everyone down the stairs and out to his truck.

"Really," Maggie insisted. "Cassidy and I can walk to the school. We always do."

"We're already late," Matt protested.

"I want to walk," Caleb volunteered.

"Matt's right," Jared said. "We're already late. Plus, there's something I'd like to ask you. I don't know if I'll have another chance to get away."

Jared's sons quickly piled in the backseat. Matt and Ryan sat by the coveted windows, while Caleb was more than annoyed to be in the middle. Cassidy, looking way too pleased, climbed in the front, quite content to be in the middle. She snapped on her seat belt and looked at Jared as if he were Santa, the Tooth Fairy and the Easter Bunny all rolled into one. Jared knew the look well. It usually meant the kid using it was about to ask for something.

"Why don't you have a girl?" Cassidy asked, once he'd put on his own seat belt and started the truck.

The snort from the backseat might have been Ryan or

might have been Matt. For the first time, Jared got what Grandpa Billy meant when he said *the apple didn't fall far from the tree.* It was all Jared could do not to snort, too. The only obvious non-snorter was Caleb because the five-year-old said, "Yeah, Dad, I want a sister. We can name her Molly."

"We don't need a—" Jared stopped, suddenly realizing that not just one but both females in the front seat were staring at him.

"We have a girl," Jared revised. "Her name is Beth, and she'll have to be in charge of giving you girl relatives."

"But—" Caleb started to say.

Jared held up one hand. "End of conversation."

"Dad has to be married in order for there to be a sister," Ryan told Caleb.

"And Dad doesn't like girls," Matt added.

Jared almost drove off the road. Where did Matt get that idea? As for Maggie, she was looking away from him and out the window. He could tell by the way her cheeks were sucked in and her lips were puckered, that she was doing all she could not to laugh.

"Why don't you like girls?" Cassidy asked.

"I do like girls," Jared assured her, "especially ones who eat blueberry pancakes and ones who show me exactly where to park."

Cassidy giggled and pointed to a visitor's spot right by the front walkway of Roanoke Elementary. "Am I a visitor?" Jared asked.

"Yes," Cassidy decided. "Because you're not a kid and you don't work here."

"Good enough," Jared agreed.

A moment later, both he and Maggie had signed their children in as tardy and watched as all of them, clutching late slips, scurried to their classrooms.

Well, Matt didn't scurry. He looked at Jared accusingly.

The only thing worse than being late, to Matt's way of thinking, was being late alongside Cassidy Tate.

Jared had never stopped at Roanoke's only coffeehouse just to have coffee. What he was paying for two cups could buy a whole pound, not that he would have. He didn't like coffee. Plus, the concept of just sitting around, doing nothing, felt strange. He resisted the urge to fidget.

"You always come here after dropping Cassidy off at school?" He shifted in the brown hardback chair and stretched out his legs. They didn't fit under the tiny table.

Maggie took a sip of something that was more chocolate than coffee and nodded. "As often as I can. It's my one treat before I open the store for the day. Usually, though, I'm alone so I sit here and write in my journal. Or I read. Do you like to read?"

He hadn't been asked that question in almost fifteen years, not since high school. "I read the Bible."

"Oh."

She visibly recoiled, her withdrawal so tangible it made him stop thinking about where to put his feet and how much he'd paid for the stupid cups of coffee.

"When I have time," he added, hoping to get her to relax, "I read the newspaper."

"Online or paper?"

"A little bit of both."

Instead of looking at Maggie and trying to figure out why his reading the Bible could put such a look of vulnerability—or fear?—on her face, Jared took a drink of his coffee. Bitter stuff, downright nasty. Good thing the cup wasn't that big.

He decided to get right to the point. "Beth has pretty much insisted that I come talk to you."

"And here I thought you just stopped by because you knew I needed help with breakfast."

When she smiled, it about made him want to forget the

real reason he had stopped by. But, only for a moment. "She thinks you can give me some ideas on how to help my son Caleb. He's having trouble at school."

Maggie was already nodding. "I told Beth she could send anyone my way. When Cassidy started having trouble in school, I felt so alone. My husband wasn't around and when he was, he didn't really understand. For months my only friends were the specialists and the books and articles I was reading practically every night on how to deal with Attention Deficit."

He looked at her empty ring finger and desperately tried to remember what Joel had said about why a Mr. Tate wasn't around.

"I'm not sure that anything is wrong with Caleb," Jared said finally. "I think I just need to be stricter and—"

He knew the moment he lost her. Her smile flattened. Her stare was suddenly focused on something other than his face. His late wife, Mandy, used to get the same look on her face, usually when he was saying something about why the living room wasn't picked up or why they were having hamburger for the third night in the row. It was only when Mandy got sick and couldn't do anything that he realized just how much she'd been doing.

And how clueless he'd been.

"Look," he backtracked, "Caleb is just five. He lost his mother when he was not yet two, and he pretty much lost me for almost a year. That he can focus at all is a miracle. I want to be a good dad. Beth says you have more parenting tips than Dr. Spock."

He was trying to be nonchalant, but he was out of his comfort zone. He was used to women who wore comfortable shirts tucked into jeans. She wore enough pink to be a flamingo. She didn't look old enough to be a parent, let alone one who gave advice when the going got tough.

"The most important thing I can tell you is don't be afraid

to ask for help, take all the advice that is offered and also be willing to sacrifice to get it."

"Sacrifice?"

She nodded. "Time mostly."

Something Jared didn't have in abundance.

"You asked me for advice," Maggie reminded him. "Funny, but it all goes back to something we talked about the first time in Beth's classroom. Here's the truth. When dealing with Caleb, patience isn't a virtue, it's your only barrier between sanity and chaos."

Great, Jared thought, because if he remembered correctly, she had told him, upon that first meeting, that patience was *seldom* found in a woman and *never* in a man.

"I was really hoping," he said, "that you'd give me some concrete advice. You know, an earlier bedtime, maybe he needs to eat more fruit." Jared was grasping at straws and trying to remember everything he'd looked for on the internet.

She shook her head. He had an idea that whatever concrete advice she gave would be hard, harder than he could do.

"An earlier bedtime is always good. What kind of advice do you really want? I mean, is Caleb having trouble finishing homework? Sleeping? Does he worry a lot?"

Unfortunately, the only thing that didn't ring true was worry. Caleb didn't have a care in the world, especially when it came to homework.

"He gets stomachaches more than my other two and spends more time in the bathroom. Other than that, he's a normal kid." Thankfully the cell phone he'd never wanted and now couldn't live without saved him from having to say anything else. He wasn't prepared for her questions, and he knew her advice would be near impossible to follow.

"This is Jared," he answered. It only took a moment to hear about the latest catastrophe facing those in charge of the church party.

"Absolutely," Jared promised. "I'll head home now and get some more." Never before had he been glad to hear that he hadn't brought enough hay for a maze. By now, he should be an expert on mazes.

He couldn't help it. After he disconnected the call, he checked his watch again.

This meeting was over.

And Maggie Tate was looking at him as if he'd disappointed her.

For some reason, it bothered him.

"Mom, Mom, Mom." Cassidy rarely said *Mom* only once. She usually said it three or more times just because she could.

"I'm getting dressed."

"But I'm ready. Did you know that this outfit would look much better with red boots?" Cassidy didn't expect an answer. She just looked at the two presents under the tree: one really small, the other really big. Neither looked the size of cowboy boots.

Maggie was no dummy. She'd wrapped the cowboy boots in a box five times their size.

"For now, your regular shoes will have to do. And, Cassidy, if you keep interrupting me, we'll be late."

Cassidy had put on her good clothes the moment she had gotten home and had been chanting "I'm ready" for almost three hours.

Maggie applied a layer of red lipstick that matched the red of her Norma Jean wool-blend winter dress. The weatherman predicted snow, and although it hadn't arrived yet, cold temperatures had. Maggie wanted to be prepared for the worst and a fully lined frock would do the trick.

At least on the outside.

The inside, *her insides,* had a completely different need—one that pretty clothes couldn't mask. She'd not stepped foot in a church for a year, not since Dan died.

It's not a church service, Beth had insisted. *It's just a party. No Bible study and we'll be singing Christmas songs.*

It wasn't Beth's invitation that was getting Maggie to church. It was Cassidy's, "But, Mom, all my friends will be there."

It's not a church service, Maggie told herself. *And even if it turns into one, I can just take a bathroom break.*

Maggie's biggest fear was letting God get close.

Because that would stir up a memory Maggie was trying desperately to bury, one that involved Dan and injustice.

"Cool," Cassidy approved when Maggie finally made it to the living room. "I'm ready."

"I feel cool," Maggie agreed. Only, really, she didn't. Ever since Jared had taken her out for coffee this morning, broached the subject of Caleb needing help—*of Jared needing help*—and then chauffeured her home, she'd felt a bit off.

As if she'd left something undone.

It was usually mothers who'd come to Maggie to ask quietly if meeting with a developmental specialist had made a difference. They'd often thrown out tidbits of how their own children were behaving as if hoping Maggie would say something like, "Oh, that's just typical kid behavior. I doubt you need to do all I'm doing."

But Maggie wasn't a specialist and wouldn't offer any advice as to what someone else's child needed. Early on, she had discovered that sometimes the mothers hoped she'd give them ideas on ways to "fix" their children.

Their children weren't broken. Cassidy wasn't broken. There was no fix. All Maggie could do is share what had worked and what hadn't worked for them.

Patience worked, but it took time. Losing her patience didn't work and took even more time.

"Mom, Mom, Mom."

"What?"

"Can I have some hot chocolate?"

"No, they're serving a meal at the party. I've already paid the five dollars, and I want you to eat real food."

"Hot chocolate is real."

"Real sugary," Maggie agreed.

"But—"

"Get your heavy coat, plus mittens. Then grab your backpack. I think there will be prizes and candy. Let's go."

She'd diverted Cassidy. Taken the child's mind off the hot chocolate and on to something else, something Cassidy wanted. End of problem.

It worked, this time.

Something else that worked for Cassidy was walking—well, Maggie walked, Cassidy skipped—to the church, waving at people who passed by.

As they turned onto Calver Street, Maggie could see the Main Street Church ahead. The parking lot was already fairly full. A few stragglers were exiting their cars. In the back, she could see the hay bale maze Jared and his crew had been working on. A campfire was already burning. Plus, she could also see a horse pulling a wagon full of kids.

Good thing the storm was holding off and the weather was cold but not freezing.

Near the wagon ride was Jared's big black truck, tailgate down, and even though the festival was starting, a group of men were still unloading bales of hay.

All day long she'd been thinking about the man, how his presence had filled her kitchen, how wonderful all the noise had been, and—

"Caleb told me about this maze. His uncle, Joel, designed it. They started it yesterday, but something happened and they had to fix it. I think Matt's daddy didn't bring enough hay the first time. He had to go back for more."

Aah, that's why coffee and conversation was cut short.

They reached the parking lot and hurried toward the entrance.

The horse neighed, a distant sound that echoed in the early-evening chill and beckoned Cassidy. "Mom, Mom, Mom. That's what I want to do first!" She sped up, her hand automatically reaching back for her mother and dragging Maggie along.

That's when Jared McCreedy exited the front door of the church, Caleb's small hand in his. Caleb was dragging his feet, practically falling in an effort to halt his father's progress. A constant stream of "No, No, No" came from his mouth. Heading to the side of the building, away from the crowd of people, Jared bent down and starting talking.

Maggie couldn't hear the words, but she knew by Caleb's bowed head that somehow the little boy had gotten in trouble. And Jared McCreedy was doing what good fathers across the world do. He was shepherding. He was offering wisdom. He was trying to teach right from wrong.

As Maggie entered the church, she could imagine Caleb arguing with his dad. It didn't take any imagination at all to picture Jared. He wouldn't be open to an argument, especially coming from his youngest son.

"Welcome, we're glad you could join us!"

Maggie shelved her musings about Jared for a moment and smiled at the woman greeting them. Upswept hair, perfect makeup and wearing an outfit that could have come right out of Maggie's store.

"Is that Lilli Ann?" Maggie asked.

The woman turned. "Where?"

"I mean the designer of your vintage suit."

The woman checked her outfit. "Oh, this is just something I threw on. My sister sent it from Des Moines a few years ago. She said it just looked like something I'd wear."

Too bad. So far in Roanoke there'd not been a true fashionista who could talk Crepe Fox Fur or gold-tone pearl buttons.

Safe topics for in a church foyer when you really didn't
want to be there.

"Let me take your coats," the woman offered.

It's not a church service, Beth had insisted. *It's just a
party. No Bible study and we'll be singing Christmas songs.*

"No," Maggie insisted. "We're fine. I'll hang them up."
If she hung up her cocoa leather and shearling coat, she'd
know right where to get it if she needed a quick getaway.

Not that her coat could get lost amid the heavy leather
jackets and box-store offerings hanging on the rack. None of
tonight's attendees seemed to be into double-breasted fronts
and huge collars.

"Have you been here before?"

Maggie knew what was coming next: an invitation to
services.

"Excuse me." Maggie pulled Cassidy in front of her. "We
need the restroom."

"Right over there."

After a thorough washing of her hands—not because they
were dirty but because Maggie needed to get her bearings—
and several deep breaths, all while Cassidy urged "Come
on, Mom, Mom, Mom, pleeeeeease," Maggie headed for the
foyer again. The woman who'd greeted her was already at
the door with some other victim.

"There's a horse," Cassidy reminded.

"Perfect." The horse was outside. To Maggie's way of
thinking, being outside a church was much better than inside a church.

As they made their way to the line for the horse and wagon
rides, first picking up plastic cups of hot chocolate, Maggie
noticed that Jared and Caleb were still standing at the side
of the church.

Cassidy, though, was all about Cassidy. In a nanosecond,
Maggie was holding both their drinks while Cassidy charged

full speed ahead. She would have made it, too, if a toddler hadn't suddenly veered in her way.

Cassidy recalculated, turned left, stumbled, went down, seemed momentarily stunned, but then hopped up and without so much as a backward glance at the toddler who had deterred her, got in line.

It was that magical seven-year-old energy.

Nope, Maggie thought for the second time, she wouldn't change a thing about Cassidy. Every nuance was part of the precious package that Maggie loved, unconditionally.

Looking behind her, she watched Jared with his son. At one time, Maggie had been a prayer warrior. If that were still true, she'd be praying that Jared McCreedy was the kind of father who would soon figure out the same thing about his youngest son.

But Maggie no longer prayed. She'd seen firsthand the power of answered prayers and it terrified her.

Chapter Four

The Main Street Church certainly drew a crowd. Maggie recognized customers, parents of Cassidy's classmates and even Henry Throxmorton, the owner of the antiques store from across the street who never seemed to smile. He wasn't smiling now, but he was sitting at a table across from two other men—both knew how to smile—and looking as comfortable as she'd ever seen him. His wife, looking frail but content, sat next to him.

Only six months in Roanoke and already she knew a few faces. For the first time since entering the church doors, Maggie relaxed. She could do this.

Maggie quickly purchased a few tickets and followed the path Cassidy had already taken—sans the toddler. How Cassidy knew her way around, Maggie didn't know. In a matter of minutes, they were both in line for the horse and wagon. Never mind the cold! There were a handful of adults and a crush of kids under ten, most of whom Maggie did not know, but Cassidy did.

With mittens on and hats down over their ears, Cassidy and Maggie rode in the wagon bed, singing Christmas songs at the top of their lungs along with anyone else foolhardy enough to be outside in the freezing weather.

Joel McCreedy, Jared's brother, added a deep bass from his position at the reins. He listened to the kids' suggestions for songs, told jokes and even paid attention as little ones shouted their lists for Santa Claus.

Joel was easygoing, not like his older brother. With a devil-may-care glint in his eyes and I-can-do-anything attitude, the younger McCreedy brother had quickly won over both Maggie and Cassidy this past summer while he worked on remodeling the store that became Hand Me Ups.

Still, it was the older brother that Maggie couldn't seem to forget.

After three go-rounds, the cold soon drove the Tate women inside to the crowded fellowship hall where the food smelled as inviting as the people were. It only took a moment before Cassidy claimed she was warm again and stood at one of the large windows staring longingly at the horse toting around yet another group of revelers.

Not a chance. Maggie was so cold her teeth hurt.

"Joel said that when the crowd dies down, I can sit up front with him. Then it would be fair." Cassidy stood so close to the window that her breath frosted the glass.

Maggie was no dummy. "Which means we'll be here until cleanup."

"Yes," Cassidy said brightly.

Just as Maggie was ready to open her mouth, squash that idea—

"We can always use help with cleanup."

Trust Beth Armstrong to walk by at just the right moment. Her arms were full of paper plates, cups and napkins. Matt McCreedy followed her with a stack of plastic forks. He tripped over his untied shoelaces and the forks hit the ground. Maggie and Cassidy gathered them up and followed Beth and Matt to the kitchen.

"I'm not quite sure where Jared's gotten off to." Beth

joined the workers in the kitchen. "He's supposed to be helping with serving. He never shirks his duty."

"Dad's busy," Matt volunteered.

"Doing what?"

Matt gave the typical kid reply. "I don't know."

Maggie bit her lower lip. She knew how busy Jared was.
She also believed Beth's words about Jared and responsibility. Her husband had been like that, putting duty first. Could
be Jared had lost all track of time and didn't realize how cold
it was. If Jared and Caleb were outside, then maybe now was
the perfect time to start interfering.

Helping.

She wasn't interfering.

"Watch Cassidy for just a moment, will you?"

In response, Beth set Cassidy to putting plastic dining
ware into separate containers.

Stepping outside the kitchen and once again into the fellowship hall, Maggie quickly looked around. No Jared. She
headed for the foyer, still full of people in varying stages
of taking off coats, putting them back on. Most laughing.
No Jared.

She really hadn't been expecting to find him in either
place.

Then, exiting the church, she rounded the corner and
found both Jared and Caleb leaning against the building,
both of them looking half-frozen.

"We'll go in when you calm down," Jared was saying.

"Noooooooo."

Maggie had to give Jared credit, he didn't lose his temper
at Caleb's belligerent whine nor did he give in. His voice,
however, was sharp when he said, "I'm sure getting cold."

"Noooooooo." If anything, the whine got louder. Jared
winced and stood his ground.

"I'll bet you're getting hungry, too," Maggie announced

as she rounded the corner, hoping she was doing the right thing, slightly nervous at intervening.

Helping, she was helping.

She wished someone had been around when she was first going through this.

"Cassidy's been looking for you, Caleb." Maggie looked at Jared, trying to gauge whether he wanted her help or wanted her to back off. His expression was unfathomable. But, judging by the way he gritted his teeth, he did need help—whether he wanted it or not.

"Seems your Uncle Joel has promised a hayride with a couple of kids sitting up front," Maggie continued. "She thought you'd like to go with her."

Happiness for a moment, back to anger and then doubt all flickered across Caleb's face.

"That would be fine with me," Jared encouraged. His hands were shoved deep in the pockets of his tan coat. A black knit cap was pulled over his head, low enough so Maggie couldn't see his eyes, but not so low that it did a good job of protecting his face.

Caleb pushed himself away from the church, a little clumsily since he had on a heavy coat—just like his father's but definitely a size too big—and boots that were also a little too big for his feet. It looked like hand-me-downs were alive and well at the McCreedy house. Without a backward glance, Caleb trotted toward the horse and wagon.

Maggie turned. She needed to get Cassidy pronto.

"Wait!" Jared said.

"Just let me get Cassidy out there to meet him. It's important that I keep my word." She hurried inside, fetched Cassidy, and rushed toward the horse and wagon.

A moment later, she promised Joel that she'd have the children's tickets after he made the round. Caleb, used to both the wagon and Joel, hopped right up on the front seat. Cassidy scrambled alongside him. Both children shouted *Giddy up!*

Maggie headed to the side of the church, albeit hesitantly. Thanks to his winter hat, she'd not been able to read his expression and wasn't one hundred percent sure he'd appreciated her interference.

Her help.

But Jared—sensible man—had already gone inside and was taking his place carrying hot dog buns to the serving area. No way did Maggie want to talk to him amid all these people.

There was a short line at the table where two women sold tickets. A jar with money inside had a photo of a family and in black marker were the words: all proceeds to go to needy families.

Nostalgia, unwelcomed and unwanted, hit Maggie like a surprise kick to the back of the knees. Three years ago, she'd been the church woman sitting at the table collecting the money. Sixteen years ago, she'd been a member of the "needy family" club.

Maggie took a deep breath. Tonight she was close to being the needy family again and as far away from the church woman as she could possibly be.

It's not a church service. It's just a party. We'll be singing Christmas songs.

But Maggie could never forget, no matter how she tried to place her memories of Christmas on a back burner for Cassidy's sake.

Christmas was not the best time to venture inside a church, and not because they collected for needy families and not because Maggie no longer prayed.

It was because it had been a December day that she'd received word that her husband had been killed in the line of duty. It had also been a December day that Maggie's mother had walked out on her daughter and husband.

I'm strong. I can do this. I will do this.

Maggie managed to buy the tickets with minimal words

and—her legs still feeling weak—backed away from the table and just stood in the middle of the crowd looking at the walls.

I'm strong. I can do this. I will do this.

The walls behind the ticket sellers were awash with Christmas drawings made by the kids. Santas of varying sizes, some even skinny, tumbled across the walls. Snowmen chased them. Snowflakes, some resembling pumpkins, came in amazing colors.

Cassidy didn't have an offering on the wall as Maggie didn't let her attend church.

Maggie left the fellowship hall. She needed something to chase away the memories of the past. She needed away from all the "Merry Christmases." It was somewhat calmer in the hallway. The Bible classroom doors were shut, but the area teemed with people and, yes, their minds were on Christmas.

Tables were set up, and a craft business seemed to be thriving. Joel could wait a little longer for the tickets. And, she knew if she wasn't there when he finished the round, he'd just take the kids again.

Low on funds, Maggie bypassed the spiral-bound cookbooks that were for sale next to a display of beaded jewelry and went straight to some knitters and crocheters who might consider selling their goods on consignment in her shop. What she really wanted was crocheted soda can hats, but she'd make the request after seeing which of the crafters wanted to work with her.

While the ticket takers on the inside were collecting money for needy families, the crafters were all about collecting money for the church camp. They were thrilled at having another avenue to make money.

There was also a husband and wife team selling photo identification badges for kids. He was flanked by an artist and a clockmaker. If she'd had some spare cash, she'd buy a few presents.

Maybe next year they'd let her set up an area and sell

vintage clothes. She could do a great business in the kids department.

That did it. Just a few thoughts about work and next year. Some of Maggie's anxiety ebbed. Enough so that when Cassidy came barreling around the corner shouting, "I couldn't find you!" Maggie was able to pick up her daughter and swing her saying, "I'll never wander far. You'll always be able to find me."

Cassidy didn't know how true those words were. She also wasn't willing to slow down to look at such grown-up temptations as jewelry and identification tags.

"How did you get away from Joel?" Maggie asked.

"We went around three times and then Joel said for Caleb's big brother to bring me to you," Cassidy explained. "There were lots of kids in line. We weren't being fair."

The sound of laughter and the smell of food wafting from the fellowship hall were a magnet. Cassidy pulled Maggie through the door and into the room crowded with people both eating and playing games.

Maggie wasn't a bit hungry.

Neither apparently was Cassidy, except for wanting a bag of popcorn which she didn't get.

In the back of the fellowship hall there was a coloring table, a face-painting table manned by Beth, and a fishing game. Cassidy looked, paused, and passed by saying, "Maybe I'll get my face painted, later."

Outside, the cold slapped at Maggie's face. Cassidy zoomed to the maze and latched on to the McCreedy boys, to both Ryan and Caleb's joy and Matt's consternation. After one turn making their way through the labyrinth, Maggie knew why. Ryan was overjoyed because he surrendered Matt and Caleb into Maggie's supervision. He disappeared with his friends toward an impromptu football game played with bigger boys and a few fathers.

Caleb was overjoyed because he just plain liked girls, Cassidy especially.

"Nothing makes Matt happy," Cassidy confided after their third time going through the maze.

"I want to go help Beth," Matt said.

Maggie looked in through one of the windows. Beth had a line ten kids deep. "Beth's busy at the face-painting booth," Maggie said. "We'll see if the line dies down soon, and then you can go help her."

An hour later, Cassidy and the boys were out of tickets and Maggie was guiding them back to the fellowship hall and the food line. Matt and Caleb ran ahead, Cassidy on their heels. Maggie wasn't quite as fast. But, the closer she got, the slower her feet became.

Once again, Jared had a towel in his hand and was cleaning up a mess. Only this time it wasn't pancake batter. It was ketchup.

She didn't have time to look away before he glanced up and caught her staring.

She could only hope he realized that she was fixated on the ketchup spill and not him.

Too bad hot dogs were a staple at Solitaire Farm because after tonight, Jared wasn't sure he could stomach the smell ever again. This wasn't his first time helping with the church's Christmas party, but it was his first time without Mandy. The last few Christmases had been hard.

Jared's helpers were ambitious and laughed a lot, but they really weren't much help. They got sidetracked on conversations, mostly football scores or whose house had been broken into recently—seemed there'd been quite a few thefts. They took too long taking orders, because every customer was a friend. They forgot where stuff was stored, even though most had attended the Main Street Church for decades and this wasn't their first time in the kitchen. And, most of all, they were clumsy.

Even worse, when they spilled things, they were more likely than not to leave the spill where it was than to clean it up.

Jared had just sent home Sophia Totwell. She had claimed a hurt ankle; he figured she was as tired of the hot dog smell as he was. Plus, she'd seen her husband and two kids wandering around, looking lost.

"I wish you'd talk to him," Sophie said to Jared as she untied her apron. "You've been farming a long time. Give him some advice on how to make money as well as spend it."

Kyle Totwell didn't want to hear what Jared had to say. He'd moved onto a broken-down farm, purchased way too many cows for his ability and finances, and was now suffering.

"Dad, can I have a hot dog?" Caleb skidded under the table, managing to rearrange the tablecloth and knock a handful of napkins to the ground. Matt picked them up and stayed on the correct side of the food counter.

"One hot dog, no bun, coming up," Jared said. He nudged Caleb around the table to stand next to Matt. He just knew his voice dripped with patience. Surely Maggie would notice how in control he was. "You want one, too?" he asked Matt.

"Yes."

"And you?" he asked Cassidy.

"I don't like buns, either."

Maggie came to the edge of the table, guiding Cassidy away from the tablecloth and smiling at Jared as if this morning hadn't happened.

"Thanks for what you did earlier, and thanks for taking my boys around," he said.

"They were no problem. We had fun."

He'd noticed. Maybe that's why he'd been so attuned to

the ambitious, laughing lot in his food court. He'd been wishing he was with Maggie and the kids.

"I'm sorry I left the coffee shop so abruptly this morn—" he started.

"Nothing to apologize for," she finished. "Some topics are harder than others."

"What are you guys talking about?" Matt wanted to know.

"Grown-up talk." Jared quickly made four plates, two with just hot dogs and two with buns, potato chips and a homemade chocolate chip cookie.

"I want a choc—" Cassidy and Caleb chimed in unison.

"Only after you eat the hot dog," Maggie said. "And then only half."

"Dad, you always give me a chocolate chip cookie," Caleb complained.

"Now might be a good time to change."

Little adult that he was, Matt had already made his way to a table and was eating his hot dog, sans ketchup—before touching anything on his plate. He did not look overjoyed when Cassidy and Caleb joined him. He did, however, astutely move his plate so his cookie was out of his little brother's reach.

"How many times did they go through the maze?" Jared asked.

"I stopped counting at seven."

Jared's next words came out before he had time to think. "You have more patience than I do." Immediately, he wanted them back. Her smile slipped a little, just enough so he knew she was thinking about this morning.

She, indeed, did have patience because instead of pointing out the obvious, she simply said, "I'd better go see what the kids are doing and make sure they eat."

He watched her walk away, her hips sashaying in such

a way that Jared wondered how such an old-fashioned red dress could look so appealing.

Maybe because it wasn't the dress.

Chapter Five

It was nine and the game lines still boasted one or two kids. Cassidy leaned back in the chair, and let Beth Armstrong's paintbrush create an image on her cheek that would soon become red cowboy boots.

Beth had more paint on her than most of the kids, and she looked ready to drop.

"I take it the Christmas party's a success?" Maggie stood slightly to the side, gently swaying with Caleb on her hip, and watched as Beth created her masterpiece.

"It always is. This year seemed really good. I heard one of the women say we raised almost five hundred dollars. There was never a moment the face-painting booth didn't have a kid."

"Me, either," Maggie agreed. "There was never a time I didn't have a kid." She switched Caleb from her left arm to her right. Good thing he was a small fellow or her arms would be more on fire than they already were.

"He's sure taken to you," Beth observed.

"This morning we had a whole conversation in the car about his dad not having a girl. Caleb seemed to think they needed one."

Cassidy giggled.

"Now, you're going to have one boot bigger than the other. Don't move," Beth scolded Cassidy before turning to Maggie. "I heard all about you taking a ride in Jared's truck. Caleb is a natural reporter. You'd think the ride went on for days. Then, too, there was something about pancake batter."

"Yes," Maggie admitted, "this morning was not my finest hour by any means. A good-looking guy stops by my place and winds up doing kitchen duty because Cassidy spilled a bowl full of pancake batter."

"On accident," Cassidy asserted.

"Then, Jared takes me out for coffee, so we can talk, and I find out he doesn't drink coffee—serious flaw, by the way—and then he gets the call about some hay emergency at church so he doesn't even get to finish the coffee that he didn't like."

"I'm glad he took my advice. Jared really needed to talk to you. He probably figures suffering through a cup of coffee a small price to pay."

"We didn't really get to talk."

"Well, you must have connected somehow. Everyone in town's going to be talking about how you chauffeured Matt and Caleb around."

"My having them is more Ryan's doing." Maggie shifted, trying to get Caleb into a better grip. It had been a long time since she'd held a sleeping five-year-old. "We ran into them at the maze and he transferred the care and feeding of these small animals to me."

"We're not animals," Cassidy protested. "I'm a cowboy—I mean cowgirl."

"They're animals," Jared agreed, coming up from behind. "We're closing down, and I get to take a break before cleanup. Anybody want a last-minute hot dog? We're giving away the leftovers." He didn't look surprised when no one took him up on his offer.

Gently, he tried to take Caleb from Maggie's arms.

But Caleb, even in sleep, was already comfortable and he

wasn't letting go. His hands curled into Maggie's shirt and his head nestled tightly into her neck.

"I think he likes me," Maggie said.

"He just likes girls," Cassidy reminded her.

"Now you're going to have part of a boot all the way to your nose," Beth said. "Stop moving. I'm going to need to do some boot repairs here." She nodded toward Caleb. "Why don't you guys take him to the nursery? He'll be more comfortable. I'll finish with Cassidy while you're gone."

Jared nodded, already turning to head from the gym. Maggie followed, letting him open the doors for her. The hallway was almost empty. The crafters had packed up what was left. The stragglers were either helping with cleanup or children of the cleanup crew. Almost everyone said something personal to Jared. More than a few introduced themselves to Maggie even while raising an eyebrow.

Small towns were the same everywhere.

After a moment, they were at the nursery's door. Jared hit a dimmer switch that allowed him to adjust the light. Just able to see, he headed past a few rocking chairs, a changing table and to a crib. "He won't be happy waking up in one of these, especially if one of his brothers finds out."

"Then we won't tell them."

Maggie gently rubbed Caleb's back. He was heavy against her chest and smelled of sweat and hot dogs and little boy.

Maggie figured his father smelled of sweat and hot dogs and big boy.

"You know your way around this church," Maggie remarked as she lay Caleb down. "This nursery reminds me of a church in Lubbock. I spent many a sermon sitting in it while taking care of Cassidy."

"So you do go to church? I've never seen you here."

It was too late to erase the words. Blame them on an overload of nostalgia. Maggie tucked the blanket over Caleb. "At one time I went to church. I don't see the need now. Although, your church is lovely. I like how everyone interacts. I was never at a congregation long enough for the members to get to know me."

"I'd hate that. Why did you move so often?"

"My husband was military."

"Was?"

Maggie busied herself by brushing a strand of Caleb's hair out of his eyes and tucking him in yet again. After a moment, Jared sat in one of the rocking chairs and said, "You don't seem to have trouble fitting in. Beth thinks highly of you and so does my brother."

"They have to think highly of me." Maggie turned to face Jared. "I stock the kind of clothes Beth likes, and I paid your brother in cash for the work he did on my shop and plan for him to do more."

Jared laughed. The sound was deep and showed Maggie a side of the man she doubted many saw. Most of the time, like when he was trying to meet with his son's teacher, or clean up messy pancake batter, or drink coffee, or even push hot dogs at a church function, he came across as way too serious.

"I think I need to think highly of you, too," he confessed.

"Why?"

"I watched you with Caleb tonight. He and Cassidy were like twins, running here, running there, running everywhere. You kept them in sight, you kept them in control and never once lost your patience."

"I've had years of practice—first with my dad, who expected me to practically salute when he issued an order, and then with my late husband."

"Your husband expected you to salute?"

"It's a military thing. And, no, Dan didn't really expect me to salute. It was more like Dan expected Cassidy to follow orders like the men he led. It wasn't happening and watching him lose his patience only inspired me to keep control at all times."

"That couldn't have been easy."

Maybe it was the late hour, maybe it was the man who so needed to understand how to be patient, maybe it was just that Maggie needed to talk.

"When Dan was still alive and home on leave, Cassidy would purposely break her pencil while doing homework. She'd let the pencil roll to the ground and claim she couldn't find it."

Jared nodded.

"I'd put away all Cassidy's toys while we tried to do homework, but Cassidy was, is, just as happy playing with—and even licking—a salt shaker or just folding a work sheet into a paper airplane. She makes killer paper airplanes."

"Caleb won't sit still long enough to notice the salt shaker let alone make a paper airplane," Jared contributed. "Plus, he asks to go to the bathroom every few minutes. Once, I thought I heard him throw up."

"By the time we figured out that Cassidy had Attention Deficit behavior—not disorder, not yet—Cassidy refused to work with her father."

Jared was silent, and Maggie could only hope he was thinking: *I can't let this happen to me.*

"Dan always turned the activity into a battle, forgetting that doing battle with a five-year-old girl didn't necessarily mean there'd be a clear winner."

The single window in the nursery let in a long, gray shadow that emphasized the empty rockers, the mural of Noah's Ark on the wall and the cribs. A forgotten diaper bag was by the changing table. The room was so quiet that Maggie could hear Jared breathing.

"Tell me what to do," he finally said.

"What do you mean?"

"I mean besides learning how to find time and balance it with patience, tell me what to do. I'm committed. I want to help my son. I appreciated you interfering earlier—"

"I wasn't interfering. I was helping." In a moment, she'd opened her purse, and took out a piece of paper and wrote down the name of two books. "Here are the titles of the two books that helped me the most. Call me if you have any questions. I don't have the right answers, and believe me, I made plenty of mistakes. But I can tell you what works best for Cassidy and me."

Jared nodded and took the paper from her hand. His fingers were warm against hers. His eyes sincere. But, in the back of her mind, she could see Dan looking just as sincere, hear Dan saying the same thing, *Tell me what to do. I'm committed. I want to help.*

Problem was, Maggie'd had a lifetime of watching people fail who claimed to be committed: first her mother and then her husband.

At least this time the person destined to fail wasn't someone Maggie loved.

Early Saturday morning, after chores and while the rest of his family still slumbered, Jared got on the computer—for once his high-speed internet actually worked—and ordered the books Maggie had suggested. He followed that with about twenty minutes of finding the perfect directions for building a hay feeder.

Time and patience, Maggie had said.

December on Solitaire Farm meant a bit more time: time to do all the things, like building a hay feeder that Jared had put off during the busy season. The best thing about this feeder was the cost, possibly under five dollars. It could be built out of scrap plywood. What he didn't use, he'd take to the school for props. He hadn't planned to start the feeder today, but after last week with Caleb getting sent to the office and then the conference with his teacher, and then last night with Maggie, well, Jared had plenty to think about.

Since there was nothing to plow, and he had lots of thinking to do, he needed to do something with his hands.

Already fully dressed, Jared merely put on his heavy parka and hat before heading for the barn. There was a slight misting of ice on the porch. The soles of his work boots barely noticed. The cold air momentarily stung his hands and he buried them in his pockets. According to the almanac, winter wouldn't arrive for another three weeks, but God's timeline didn't care what was predicted.

Jared's father had been a master at predicting snow. He'd laughed when Jared asked how. The same man who'd taught Jared "Always plow around stumps," had also advised, "If a cat washes her face o'er the ear, 'tis a sign the weather will be fine and clear." He'd followed that with, "When clouds look like black smoke, a wise man will put on his cloak."

Stepping off the bottom porch step, Jared turned and looked at the home he'd grown up in. It was all his now, since Joel had sold his share right out of high school. Owning a farm was a lot of work. Some of Jared's neighbors hadn't quite figured that out. There were a lot of wannabes moving in, like the Totwells who'd purchased an old farm just five miles east of Solitaire Farm. They'd named it Roanoke Creek even though they didn't have a creek. The father, Kyle Totwell, was always showing up on Jared's door with questions. Fool kid—same age as Joel—purchased cows, lots of cows, before he knew how to care for them.

Jared was primarily an Iowa row crop farmer. He raised a few animals because his father had, but scaled way back—just what his family needed. Joel was set on changing that. Joel liked the live-animal part of farming, like Kyle Totwell did.

There was something amusing about a family who thought farming a romantic profession, a way to get back to nature. The smell of manure was as back to nature as one could get. As for romantic...there was nothing romantic about getting up at four in the morning, dressing in the dark so as to not wake anyone and then heading out into the cold.

Jared couldn't imagine doing anything else, living anywhere else, but since Mandy died, the fear of failure—not having enough time and not having enough heart—had settled like a seed in his stomach that sprouted, grew, retracted, only to hibernate just waiting for the opportunity to rear its head again.

"Dad, I sure wish you were here now."

It had been a while since Jared had paid lip service to his dad's memory. The last time had probably been the day after Mandy's death when he'd found himself on his knees next to their bed, now his alone, and Jared had beat the sheets with his fists, silently screaming, "Why? Why? Why?"

He, like a child, had wanted his dad that day. His dad would have been the only one who would have chanced entering the bedroom, would have known the words to say when, really, there were no words.

Jared tore away his eyes from the two-story farmhouse that housed his sleeping family, a family that depended on him.

Depended on him not to fall victim to the winter doldrums.

Hands in his pockets, Jared walked across the yard. His dog, Captain Rex, named by one of the boys, came from wherever he'd been and settled companionably alongside. Except for an occasional sound from where the cows stood, the Iowa morning was silent.

Silent and cold.

Almost every farmer Jared knew experienced winter frustration. Most worked jobs off the farm to keep things going. Jared hadn't wanted to, so he'd done the next best thing. He'd opened a small market at the edge of the property right where the rural road met the intersection into town. It had been Mandy's idea, and she'd kept it up when she was alive.

Billy had helped after Mandy's death. It provided some income, not much. Then, last year, Joel finally realized he was needed at home.

Joel was a natural shopkeeper as well as a gifted carpenter and took Solitaire's Market to a new level. He pretty much changed the shed Solitaire's Market was occupying into a log cabin that sold more than produce. His girlfriend, Beth, Caleb's teacher, had a say. So, along with some very non-farm items, like oil paintings and homemade soap, Jared now met the needs of his customers' children. For a mere dollar, they could travel through a real corn maze. The maze at last night's church Christmas party was nothing compared to the permanent one next to Jared's—make that Joel's—store.

To Jared's amazement, people came from as far as Knoxville. Just a few weeks ago, Joel and Beth had decorated the maze for Thanksgiving. Fake turkeys, cardboard pilgrims and Indians, and a giant cornucopia were all part of the experience. When kids and their parents exited, they were given an ear of Indian corn with a tag advertising Jared's farm tied to the end. He made almost as much money on the maze as he did selling pumpkins and other produce. And, he wouldn't have sold as many pumpkins without the maze.

He turned on the light in the barn. This was one of the few places where Mandy's ghost behaved. She'd helped out here, sure, but not very often. Her place had been inside and with the boys.

Which is now my place, Jared reminded himself. Being both mom and dad wasn't easy, but it was rewarding, and yes, it was getting easier—thanks to Beth.

Beth, Mandy's best friend.

Beth had been around forever, first helping with Jared's wedding, then baby showers and finally when Mandy got sick.

Jared had been busy working the farm. He'd accepted whatever Mandy wanted.

Now, he wished he'd chosen time with Mandy over time on the farm. The farm was silent and cold, nothing like the companionship of his warm and sensitive wife. But this was Jared's life now, and with a quick prayer, he left those thoughts behind and got to work.

Chapter Six

"But I want a real tree, real tree, real tree." Cassidy was in rare form. Last night had ignited her energy level and today she'd hit the ground running and hadn't stopped. Luckily, the patrons of Hand Me Ups had been in the Christmas spirit and fairly understanding. Although Maggie heard one older woman mutter something about *be good or else Santa won't...*

Cassidy either hadn't heard the prediction or had pretended not to hear. Sometimes Maggie couldn't tell.

"Real tree," Cassidy said yet again.

Maggie sat behind the counter and pushed a needle into an elf's hat. She'd promised to make fifty and was on number thirty-nine. They were easy, but fifty turned out to be more time consuming than she'd figured. Cassidy's chanting didn't help. Maggie ignored each and every pronouncement, even though they'd gotten louder each time. Things like money and convenience didn't really matter to Cassidy, yet. Someday they would. "I know, but our place isn't that big and real trees cost more."

"You need two trees," Cassidy decided, looking around the store. "We can get a little one, like you want, for upstairs, cuz you're right. It's small up there. But downstairs here in your shop, we can put up a real one, real one, real one."

Most of the shops had put up their Christmas trees the day after Thanksgiving. When Maggie and Cassidy got back from New York, the street had been transformed.

The bell above the door jangled as Beth Armstrong came in.

Cassidy took one look at the box in Beth's arms and said, "Yes, a big tree, and we can hang Miss Beth's soap like they're ornaments. That will help sell them."

"Not a bad idea," Beth said.

Maggie knew when she was outnumbered and wisely kept silent. A Christmas tree was just a tree, nothing else, no need to think it stood for anything but a decoration.

Still, Cassidy knew the exact moment she'd won the battle and ran for Beth, almost knocking over the woman. "I am so happy!" Turning to her mother, she asked, "When can we get them? Can they be real? Please."

"Maybe we'll go tonight, and we'll probably get them at Bob's Hardware. It's what we can afford."

Beth made a face. "Bob's Hardware. Ack."

"You know as well as I know that there are only two places in town selling imitation trees. I can't afford the novelty store. Bob's trees are reasonable."

"They're not even made at the North Pole," Beth muttered.

"Then where are they made?" Cassidy asked.

"We're changing the subject before I change my mind," Maggie said.

Luckily, a customer came through the door at that moment, and Maggie didn't have to say anything else. Cassidy was quite willing to take up the slack.

"Mommy doesn't have any new wedding dresses for you to look at."

"That's okay." Beth looked at Maggie. "Joel's got something to do tomorrow after church. I thought we could head to Fairfield and look at some of the antiques stores there. This close to Christmas, some of them stay open on Sundays. I've only a few weeks until the wedding. We need to find my dress, and soon."

"I want to go," Cassidy agreed.

"You could always attend ch—"

"I'm sorry," Maggie said. "I promised Sophia Totwell we'd come out to her house tomorrow afternoon. She called me this morning. She's been going through the basement and found suitcases full of old clothes. You could come with me. It's a long shot, but maybe we'd find a dress. Stranger things have happened."

"Can we do both?" Beth considered.

"We can try. Want me to pick you up at your house just after noon?"

"Sounds good," Beth agreed. Heading for one of the shelves next to the register, she added the handmade soap to her display and checked to see what had sold.

Maggie wished she could pay Beth early, but she cut the consignment checks once a month and now that it looked like the Tate women would be the proud owners of not one but two trees, Maggie needed to look again at her budget.

"It takes four years for a business to boast a profit," Maggie reminded herself.

"What?" Beth said.

"Just talking to myself."

"You're pretty good at talking," Beth commented. "You were holding your own last night with my future brother-in-law."

"We were talking kids."

"I figured that, but you got him talking and that's a feat. When Mandy died, he about crawled in a hole and stayed there." Beth's face was usually puppy-dog happy, but for a moment, a shadow crossed her features. "She was my best friend, you know."

Maggie knew. Beth was an open book.

"There wasn't a week I wasn't out there," Beth continued, "at Solitaire Farm, doing something with her family."

Maggie wasn't sure she wanted to know all this. From what she'd heard, Mandy McCreedy had died around four years ago and Jared still wasn't over her passing.

"He must have really loved her."

"Oh, he did." Beth took a notebook out of her purse, made a few notations, and then turned back to Maggie. "They started going out while she was still in junior high, too young to do anything but sit beside each other at youth-group events. He graduated before she did. Her parents said they couldn't be married until she got her high school diploma."

"Hometown favorites," Maggie said.

"Mandy was. Jared was always too grown-up to fit in with most of the high school boys. He was running the farm at sixteen."

"So," Maggie prompted, amazed by how curious she was, "the minute Mandy graduated, they got married."

"Yes and no," Beth said, leaning on the counter. "Mandy took night classes, computer classes and summer school. She graduated at midterm what should have been her junior year. If she'd have stayed, she'd have been captain of the cheerleaders and probably prom queen. Everyone loved her."

"But she loved Jared more."

"Yep. The day she got the passing grade for her final class, she told Jared even before she told her parents."

Beth wasn't done.

"That was a Friday. He proposed on Sunday. Probably the most romantic thing he'd done in his whole life."

"Proposing?"

"Yes, he did it in the foyer after church, right in front of everybody. Got down on one knee and everything. I was standing right next to Mandy's mother. No way could her parents talk to them about waiting and college after that."

"How old was Mandy?"

"Seventeen. Four years older than me."

"How'd you become best friends, then?"

Beth's cell phone sounded out a verse from "Going to the Chapel." "That's Joel. He promised to call." She punched a button, said, "I'm just on my way out of Maggie's store. Let me call you right back." Barely giving the man time to respond, she shut off the phone. "How'd we become best friends? Some things are just meant to be. Like you and me becoming friends." She closed her purse, pulled her scarf tighter around her neck and headed for the exit. "See you tomorrow."

The door banged shut behind her, but not before it let in a blast of cold air. Maggie was about to say "Brrrr," but already Beth was opening the door again.

"I'm glad you're helping him. He needs it more than you know."

Bam! Another slam of the door, another blast of cold air and then Beth was gone.

"She's pretty," Cassidy said, after the door closed. She added an afterthought, as if worried she had hurt her mother's feelings, "But not as pretty as you."

"Thank you," Maggie said. "I think."

When Maggie had opened Hand Me Ups, Beth had been her first customer. The next day, she'd brought both her sisters and a two-year-old niece. Soon Beth and Maggie were a team, always with Cassidy in tow, heading into the city and shopping. Maggie had an eye for retro and Beth had an eye for style.

Cassidy provided live entertainment.

On Saturdays and even a few evenings when Beth's fiancé was out of town, Beth had come to the shop and started sketching a mural across the back wall. In exchange, Maggie was giving Beth a discount on her wedding alterations. Beth was exactly what Maggie needed: upbeat and friendly.

Maybe, for the first time, Maggie had landed in a place where best friends did last forever. Beth was a beloved daughter, sister and town favorite all rolled up into one. She'd been born and raised here in Roanoke, only leaving to get her college degree. Maggie, on the other hand, had been an only child and army brat, spending time in Texas, Japan and Panama among other places.

When Maggie was twelve, they'd been in Hawaii. Christmas there was a bit different. Santa wore a flowered shirt for one thing, and everywhere you turned, people greeted you with *Mele Kalikimaka,* meaning Merry Christmas. While Maggie was at school, her mother had packed her belongings and walked out on the family.

She left behind presents under the tree, the last Maggie would get from her mother, and a note that said she couldn't take moving from place to place anymore.

The note hadn't explained why she couldn't take Maggie with her to just one place.

"She needs a tree."

Jared, just getting his brood rounded up for their outing, frowned at the phone. "What's keeping her from getting one?"

"Nothing," Beth said. "But, she's going to get two fake ones when two real ones would be better. Plus, since I know her finances, she'll go to Bob's Hardware in town. He only has three fake trees to choose from, and they're all lame. I know you're going tonight. You always go on the first Saturday of December. I know your schedule as well as I do my own. Call her up, and take her with you. The Deckers won't mind, and I'm sure they'll cut her a deal. I don't think she's ever had a real tree."

Jared shook his head, even though Beth couldn't see him on the other end. "There's nothing wrong with fake trees. Sometimes I think they'd be a whole lot easier."

"Then why aren't you getting one?"

She knew the answer to that. Paul Decker, his best friend from high school, owned a Christmas tree farm called Decker the Halls over in Indianola. It was a bit of a drive, but Paul and his family always made the night special for Jared's family even back when *special* didn't seem possible.

"Jared, this is her second Christmas without her husband."

"Then she's used to it." Even as the words exited his mouth, he wanted them back. They came from frustration, and yes, fear. He, more than anyone, understood the pain she was going through and it bothered him how much the idea of inviting her appealed to him.

"Call her," Beth ordered. "Or, I'll tell Joel to replace you as best man."

"Threaten me with something you'll really do."

"Ohhhh." She hung up on him.

"Dad, when are we going?" Matt, seven going on forty, stood at the bottom of the stairs. He was dressed, even to his shoes. He was Jared's little timekeeper and figured they were late.

"Thirty minutes."

"Do I have to go?" Ryan, nine but already acting like a teenager, didn't want to go, but the moment they got to the Deckers' place, Jared knew Ryan would be the one having the most fun.

Ryan stood at the top of the stairs, wearing shorts and socks, nothing else.

Paul Decker had a nine-year-old daughter who was just as good at video games as Ryan.

"Ryan!" Jared called, "Get dressed and find out what Caleb's doing."

Overhead, the sound of his oldest stomping his feet as he went from his bedroom to Caleb's echoed through the room. Ryan was a stomper.

The phone sounded.

"Hey, little bro," Jared answered.

"I can't believe you knew it was me. Did you finally break down and get call display?"

"No, but I know your fiancée quite well and I know exactly what she's thinking, which is why I can't call Maggie Tate. This time of year is just too personal. I've finally got my family back on track and, frankly, I want to enjoy the quality time with them. She just wouldn't fit."

"Maybe you need somebody who doesn't fit to shake you up a bit. And Christmas is the perfect time."

"I've had all the shaking up I need, believe me."

Jared turned down Joel's suggestion that he call Maggie Tate as easily as he'd turned down Beth's. And, like Beth, Joel hung up without a goodbye. Jared figured, judging by the indignant feminine noise coming through the connection that Beth had her hands on the phone.

What a difference a year makes. Jared could only shake his head. His little brother, the my-saddle-sits-still-for-no-one cowboy, was so over the moon about his future wife that he'd stooped to playing a second-fiddle matchmaker.

Jared had been that in love with his late wife—so in love that when she had died, he'd almost forgotten how to live. Luckily, he'd had a family to remind him. He sat down on the couch and stared at the photo over the fireplace: his family. His late wife, Mandy, stood next to him, all smiles. He wasn't smiling, but then he'd never much cared for having his picture taken. Their three boys, stair-step brothers, were in front. Ryan held a squirming Caleb.

And Matt?

Matt, who looked exactly like Jared, was smiling.

Standing up, Jared went to the den and took the latest photograph album from a shelf. Grandpa Billy was a stickler for keeping them up-to-date.

This last year, there were more than fifty photos. The kids were in most of them. There were school photos, school activities, farm activities, church activities. There were even a few of the kids just being kids around the house.

Jared was in all of six. Hmmm, he had no excuse since Grandpa Billy was the camera man.

Matt didn't smile in any of them.

Neither did Jared.

Matt looked exactly like Jared, and maybe that wasn't a good thing.

But, it was hard to smile when your heart was broken. Jared put back the newest album and reached for last year's. It was much the same. The year before that was the same. They were all the same, clear until four years ago—the year Mandy died. Lord, he hadn't opened this one in a while, and it looked like, judging by the amount of dust, no one had. And there on the first page was the same family photograph—albeit smaller—as the one in the living room.

Matt smiling.

Mandy in her rightful place, head nestled against Jared's and a hand on the shoulder of each of her biggest boys.

He'd known the moment he had sat next to Mandy Jarrett at a church Bible Bowl practice that she was everything he'd wanted. It took him three months to work up the courage to ask if he could call. It took three phone calls—very short because he'd never been one for idle chitchat—before he finally asked her out. Their first date had been out to dinner with her parents.

He'd never been so uncomfortable in his life.

Their second date had been with his mom, Billy and Joel. It had gone a little easier because Joel carried the conversation.

Finally, after six months of parental supervision—okay, she'd been all of fifteen—they'd gone out for ice cream, just the two of them. He'd picked her up in his truck and they had a whole hour before he had to have her home.

He'd never been so comfortable in his life.

Not a chance that Maggie Tate would be a comfortable date. She'd be talking clothes and school and whether or not peanut butter could adequately stick a lunch box to a ceiling. She knew nothing about crops, football or weather cycles.

If he did invite her to come along to get a Christmas tree, what would they talk about in the truck?

Oh, Lordy, he remembered the last time she and her daughter were in the truck with him and the boys. One of the topics had been whether Jared liked girls.

No, little Miss Maggie could take care of her own tree.

She didn't need him to take her mind off a Christmas without a spouse.

"You going to sit there all night and think about calling her?" Billy came into the room, a paperback book tucked under his arm and Captain Rex at his feet. Only sixty, Billy had retired the year Mandy died. He'd taken over caring for the three boys when Jared had needed help. Today, thanks to Joel, he was more than a caregiver. He was whipping the house into shape for Joel and Beth's wedding. More than anyone, Billy knew how hard Jared worked, how hard Jared tried and how deeply Jared cared.

"Or," Billy continued, "are you going to go upstairs and round up the boys again. They've done gotten ready and now have forgotten what it is you promised them."

"No, we haven't!" Matt shouted.

"Yes, we have!" Ryan added.

"Wonder what Caleb is up to. I'll go check. Give you a little time to make the call."

"How did you—? Oh, never mind." Jared didn't want to know. "Tell them we leave in thirty minutes."

Billy nodded approvingly but said, "You're going to be late."

Jared hated being late. It took just a moment before Jared

pulled out his calendar and the odds and ends of papers he collected there.

Maggie Tate's number was on top.

He'd call, but he really hoped she'd say no.

Chapter Seven

The reason Maggie said yes had to do with her daughter, sitting across the kitchen table all big-eyed, hopeful and promising to eat every last bite of her spaghetti. To Cassidy, going anywhere with kids was better than going anywhere alone and twenty times better than staying home, especially on a Saturday evening in December.

Maggie remembered feeling the same way. Only if her mother noticed, she didn't care. As for her father, if he noticed, he didn't have the time to oblige.

"We're only getting one tree," Maggie cautioned, "for downstairs. Your idea for hanging up Miss Beth's soap as ornaments was a good one."

"One tree," Cassidy agreed. The glint in her eyes said *we can renegotiate when we get wherever we're going.*

When Jared pulled up in front of their place, they were ready. Cassidy went flying, skidding on the slick sidewalk, and banging into the side of his truck.

Jared got out and steadied her. "You all right?"

"I always do that." Cassidy wasn't fazed. "It's fun."

Matt rolled down the window and frowned. Caleb, sitting in the back of Jared's extended cab, tried to climb over him, shouting, "I want to slide!"

By the opposite window, Ryan sat playing some sort of handheld device and didn't seem to notice.

"Am I in the front?" Cassidy asked. "Because I'd really rather sit in back with the boys."

"No," Matt said quickly.

"You can sit by me," Caleb offered.

"I'm not in the middle" was Ryan's only concern.

"Looks like you're in the front." Jared leaned down and in a loud whisper said, "But it's a lot warmer up there, and tonight's going to be plenty cold." He stepped back, appraising the Tate women and gave a nod.

Because of the snow, Maggie had added a red scarf to her cocoa leather and shearling coat. Her black boots weren't retro. Instead, they were inexpensive and warm. Maggie felt like she'd passed some sort of test.

Cassidy didn't seem to notice. Already she was scooting in the driver's seat, dripping bits of snow where Jared would be sitting. Maggie walked around to the passenger side, noting that very little traffic was out this cold Saturday evening. Good, maybe the small-town radar would miss this outing between two of its singles—one of whom was walking right behind Maggie, altogether too close. She was about to turn and ask him why when they reached her door. Without a word he opened it and held out a hand to help her up.

Wow.

Maggie couldn't remember the last time a gentleman opened a door for her.

After settling her in and closing her door, Jared got behind the wheel, silently pulled out and headed for the outskirts of town.

"Tell me again where we're going," Maggie said.

"My friend Paul Decker's place. He has a Christmas tree farm over in Indianola. His family has operated it for the past fifty years."

"We've never been to a Christmas tree farm," Cassidy said. "Are there animals, too?"

"Lots of them," Caleb answered. "More than my daddy has even."

"I'm not much on livestock," Jared admitted. "Since Joel's moved home, we've doubled the number of animals."

"Have he and Beth decided what they're going to do after they get married?" Maggie knew this was a hot topic because at one time Joel had been half owner of Solitaire Farm. Since his return, Joel had worked shoulder to shoulder with Jared and profits were up, especially when it came to Solitaire's Market which, under Joel's care, had grown from a vegetable stand to a farm store.

"Not sure," was Jared's belated response.

Outside, the snow grew bigger and bolder. Inside the truck, it was dark and the smell of children and melting snow made for close quarters. Funny, Maggie usually was gripping the door handle by now. She never liked driving in snow. She never trusted anyone else driving in snow. But Jared seemed to know what he was doing and his truck, bigger than any she'd been in before, didn't seem to mind the outside conditions. Jared turned at the school and aimed his car to the emptiness of Iowa back roads.

"How long has the elementary school been at this location?" Maggie asked to break the silence.

"Since before I was born, though they've added on a time or two. This year I think they've had the highest enrollment. Billy says it's time to expand again."

"Billy?"

"Grandpa," Caleb supplied.

"You don't know Billy?" Ryan made it sound like a personality flaw.

"Watch your tone," Jared cautioned before adding, "Billy Staples. He's my stepfather and spent thirty plus years as principal of Roanoke Elementary. He helps at Solitaire Farm now. He takes care of the boys while I work."

Maggie watched as the school disappeared from view. Thirty-plus years? Imagine being in one place, one job, for that long. It was aged red brick, single level, with one class per grade.

"Was he at the Christmas party last night?"

"No." Jared turned on the high beams. "He's been fighting a cold and the cold's winning."

"I've met Grandpa Billy," Cassidy said. "He comes to school sometimes and helps. Right now he's helping with the Christmas program."

Aah, the Christmas program. Billy must be the older gentleman who sometimes helped with rehearsals.

"Any of you have parts in the play?" Maggie asked the backseat.

"Ryan has a lead," Jared said proudly.

"I give away presents," Matt answered.

"No, you don't," Caleb protested. "You just stand there."

A brief scuffle took place: Caleb whined for a moment, Matt apparently took exception to being tattled on and Ryan simply uttered, "Hey!"

"Stop" was Jared's response.

Maggie decided to try a safer discussion tactic. "I've not traveled this way."

"I've been down every road in this town it seems," Jared said. "Paul's place is about an hour away."

"And we caused you to get a late start."

"We were already running late," Ryan grumbled.

It looked like Jared was about to say something, and Maggie knew it wouldn't be something Ryan really wanted to hear.

"This is my best day ever," Cassidy said.

"Me, too," Caleb agreed.

Jared's fingers opened and closed, stretching over the steering wheel. He glanced at her and gave a tight smile.

He's as nervous as me, Maggie thought.

Paul raised an eyebrow but refrained from comment as Jared escorted Maggie and their brood into the living room. A fireplace big enough to cook in dominated the room. Two huge dogs were in front of it. Caleb and Cassidy headed for the dogs. Matt stayed by Jared's side. Surprisingly, Ryan was there, too.

"Wow," Maggie said. "This room is bigger than my whole apartment."

"My granddad was one of twelve kids. They needed a big place," Paul explained. "So, you want a tour and to pick out a tree before relaxing? Or do you want to relax before the tour and the tree?"

"Tree first!" Cassidy answered, without moving from her location next to the dog. Caleb was trying to climb on board. His dog rolled to a standing position, dumped Caleb to the ground and came over to stand by Maggie, who quickly put a hand on the huge beast's head.

"Since my good friend here—" Paul nodded toward Jared "—seems to have forgotten his manners, I'll introduce myself. I'm Paul Decker and welcome to Decker the Halls."

"It's awesome," Maggie said. "I could see the lights for miles away. It made me think of what the shepherds must have seen when the star finally landed."

"The star landed?" Caleb asked. "Really, on the ground, by Jesus? Was everyone okay?"

"Everyone was fine," Ryan answered, rolling his eyes. Jared wasn't even tempted to talk about tone. "She means when they arrived to where the star stopped." Something was going on with his oldest son and Jared wasn't sure what. Granted, for the last two weeks, Caleb had been getting more than his fair share of attention, but Ryan hadn't been deprived.

"My wife and daughters are out helping the last few customers. Let's head over there before she shuts down. It's almost seven."

As they followed Paul out the door and past the trucks, Jared said, "Paul had all girls. I had all boys. Same ages and everything."

"Yes," Paul said, "but there might be a boy for me yet."

Jared stopped. "What? You're kidding."

"Just pretend I didn't tell you," Paul advised. "I know Wendy was itching to be the one to share the good news."

"Congratulations," Maggie said.

"A boy, huh." Jared's boots crunched in the snow as he walked alongside her. The Christmas trees flanked them. Maggie reached out a finger to touch a branch every now and then. Her cheeks were pink and her smile lit up her eyes.

"You ever go in the woods to get a tree?" he asked.

"Never. We always had a small fake one. After I married Dan, I bought a bigger one, but when we moved for the third time, I realized why my dad said, 'Never buy what you're not willing to pack.'"

"Huh?" Paul said.

"Military brat," Maggie explained. "Followed by military wife."

"But if you bought fresh trees, you'd not have to worry about packing."

"No, but you'd have to find the time to go and get..." Maggie stopped. "Let's just say that Christmas trees were never at the top of the list for things to do around Christmas time in my family."

A hunk of snow fell from the top of a tree and landed on her hat. Jared watched as she laughed while shaking it off. "I promise," she said, "they'll be a priority from now on."

She stopped in front of the tented area where Wendy,

Paul's wife, and his girls were doing business. One of the neighbor boys was busy netting a purchase.

"Twenty-five for a small one," Maggie whispered. "Six dollars per foot for bigger ones."

"We're not typical customers," Jared whispered back. "Paul always sells me a tree that is somehow flawed. You know, it has too much of a gap between the branches or a crooked butt."

Caleb giggled, and Jared shot him a look.

"But you said the word b—" Caleb started.

"That's right," Jared interrupted. "I said the word, but you don't get to."

Caleb put his hands over his mouth, eyes dancing, looking like he was about to explode.

"What word does he want to say?" Cassidy asked.

"Never mind," Maggie said.

"You have a problem with her taking words out of context and being silly like this at home?" Jared asked.

"No, not really."

"I've always thought it was a boy thing," Jared agreed.

Maggie raised an eyebrow. Clearly, she wasn't convinced.

Jared looked at his three boys. Cassidy stood between Caleb and Matt. Caleb was as close to her as humanly possible without knocking her over. Matt was a good four inches away. Ryan was already talking to a girl who looked close to his age. He kept shooting glances Jared's way as if checking to make sure where he was.

"I can hardly wait to find out if that is a boy thing," Paul said.

"Yeah," Jared agreed. "Who can figure out women?"

Paul chuckled. "I was talking about girls. Guess you're thinking about women."

Jared shook his head.

This time, Paul outright laughed, almost choking as he said, "About time."

* * *

Once Wendy finished with her customer, she joined them, along with a little girl just Caleb's age named Grace. She escorted them through the rows. "We have Scotch Pine, Colorado Spruce, Frasier Fir and Balsam Fir."

"They all look the same," Cassidy noted. She looked at the little girl beside her, clearly expecting an answer, but not getting one.

"That's only because it's dark," Wendy said. "If it were daylight, you'd be able to see they have their own personality. Right, Grace?"

Grace nodded and shyly smiled. That was all the encouragement Cassidy needed. Soon the two little girls were holding hands.

The women easily left the men behind. Jared was telling Paul something about the Totwells and too many cows. That conversation was designed to make the kids scatter. Only Caleb seemed inclined to keep up with the girls. He was even willing to hold hands.

"Jared said you might have some trees on discount because of gaps or crooked butts." Maggie looked at Caleb and Cassidy. Both held mittened hands over their mouth to keep from responding.

"We do have some discounted trees. Jared and Mandy—" Wendy stopped, regrouped and said, "Jared's been bringing his family here to pick out their tree for more than a decade. It's tradition."

"How much?" Maggie asked. She had thirty-two dollars in her wallet. Hand Me Ups was closed tomorrow, so there'd be no money coming in. Plus, tomorrow they were heading to the Totwell place and Maggie might be purchasing vintage clothes. She preferred to outright buy rather than consign. She made more money that way, and right now, every dollar helped.

"We can probably find you the perfect tree for about fifteen."

"Like this one?" Cassidy stopped beside a tree double her height. "It's perfect."

"That's a Scotch Pine and definitely one of the most popular. When you get it home, and in the light, you'll see how beautiful the dark green foliage is."

"I can see that already," Cassidy said proudly.

"How old are you?" Wendy asked.

Cassidy proudly said, "Seven."

"Well, so is that tree. And, indeed, that tree is only fifteen dollars."

"Oh, Mom." Cassidy practically danced. "Can we keep it forever?"

"We'll keep it as long as we can," Maggie promised. Turning to Wendy she said, "I'm going to be putting it in my shop and hanging some of the merchandise on it."

"What kind of shop do you have?"

"Hand Me Ups, vintage clothes."

"Oh, I can't believe I didn't put two and two together. Beth talks about you all the time. I've been meaning to get into town and see what you have."

"You like vintage clothes?"

"I'm more a jeans and T-shirt kind of gal," Wendy confessed, "but I'm always looking for the perfect night-on-the-town outfit in case my husband surprises me."

"Come by. Since you're giving me a discount on the tree, I'll do the same in the store unless it's one of my consignment items."

Wendy looked back at Cassidy. "She your one and only?"

"Yes. My husband died in Afghanistan last year. We'd decided to wait until he got out of the service to have another baby."

Actually, Dan had decided that, and after Cassidy had

been diagnosed with ADD, he'd stopped wanting to discuss a second child at all.

"That's tough. Jared knows how you feel. He and Mandy planned on five, same as me and Paul. She was more a jeans and T-shirt kind of gal, too. So, how long have you and Jared been going out?"

"We're not going out. Our kids are friends, and Beth pretty much convinced him that if he didn't bring me, I'd be buying a fake tree from Bob's Hardware."

Wendy shuddered. "I think Bob purchased a surplus of artificial trees back in the sixties and is still trying to foist them off on an unsuspecting public."

Maggie laughed. "An unsuspecting public would be me. Until this morning, I wasn't sure I'd even be getting a tree. Now it's going to be the centerpiece of my store."

"After you decorate the tree, call me. I'll take a picture and display it on the bulletin board in our store."

"You have a store, too?" Cassidy asked.

Grace answered, "The store has lots of candy canes."

"Among other things," Wendy said indignantly, "like tree stands, which you'll need, and wreaths, which you can buy a different year." As an aside to Maggie, she added, "Just about everyone in the area has some kind of side business, be it a store or something over the internet. We have to, in order to make ends meet." Louder, to include the kids, she said, "Let's get the men and show them your tree. It should be perfect. One thing about the Scotch Pine is the stiff branches. They'll hold up heavier items."

"Like Beth's soap," Maggie said.

"Like Beth's soap," Wendy agreed.

They led their followers back to where Jared was examining a tree even bigger than Maggie's.

Wendy said. "You guys can go ahead and cut, shake, wrap and load the trees. Jared, you bring enough blankets?"

"Matt and Ryan are fetching them now."

"Good. Maggie and I are going to go start the hot chocolate. Come to the kitchen after you've loaded everything up."

Wendy motioned for Maggie to follow. Cassidy didn't move. She stayed to make sure the men knew exactly which tree the Tate women wanted.

There was a part of Maggie that wanted to stay with the men, see what exactly happened when a Scotch Pine left the frozen ground and started its magical journey to the center of a little girl's Christmas.

Being pregnant hadn't slowed Wendy down one bit. She quickly led Maggie to a kitchen meant to feed a crowd. Soon, water was boiling and cups were set out. Wendy had a black marker—smart woman—to write names so cups didn't get mixed up.

"By the way," Wendy said, handing Maggie her hot chocolate. "Your comment about Jared bringing you because Beth convinced him to…"

Maggie took a long drink. "Yes."

"Jared doesn't do anything he doesn't want to do."

Maggie looked out the window and spotted Jared holding one end of a giant tree. Jared did seem to know his own mind, but Maggie knew he was just doing Beth a favor by helping Maggie. That's all there was to it.

Chapter Eight

They'd stayed at the Deckers' longer than Jared intended. The boys had insisted on showing Cassidy the petting zoo. Paul was another farmer always thinking about earning an extra dollar in today's economy. Wendy had insisted on showing Maggie the store. Surprise—Maggie Tate was a woman who could enter a store and leave without purchases. Then, Paul insisted on a game of UNO that turned into five games. Everyone played except Caleb. Even Grace, who was five months younger than Caleb, knew how to play and played well.

Caleb partnered up with Maggie and made it through a game and a half before losing interest and heading off to chase the dogs.

It had been ten when Jared herded his sons out the door. Maggie and Cassidy were right behind.

Possibly because Matt fell asleep almost the minute they took off, Cassidy was quiet on the ride home and leaned against Maggie. Twice Cassidy asked for the candy cane Wendy Decker had given her on the way out. Twice Maggie said no. The second time, Maggie mentioned that if Cassidy asked again, the candy cane would be put away for an undisclosed amount of time.

Caleb's candy cane was long gone. The kid devoured it in two bites. Ryan didn't like candy canes, and Matt couldn't stay awake long enough to care about his.

How could three kids be so amazingly different?

It was eleven when Jared arrived at Maggie and Cassidy's place. Snow dripped from the eaves and the lights from the street made it, thanks to all the clothes on display, look like people were inside.

"Spooky," Caleb summed it up.

Cassidy seemed to think for a moment before saying, "But it's a good spooky."

"You need Christmas lights," Jared said.

"Next year."

Maggie and Cassidy climbed in the back of the truck and pushed, trying to unload their tree. To Jared, it looked like they laughed more than pushed. Jared, Ryan and Caleb pulled. Even with Caleb's help, or maybe because of Caleb's help, it took quite a few minutes to unload the tree.

Getting it through the door of the shop was another adventure. Once inside, it became clear that although Maggie had done well in choosing the spot—away from a heat vent—the space wasn't adequate. Jared coerced Ryan into moving a few things.

"I'll help you put it up," Jared offered.

"Dad!" Ryan's voice was a bit higher than usual. Jared's lips went together and his oldest son backed off.

"You guys are tired. It's almost midnight. I can do it," Maggie insisted.

Jared perused the room. If the tree fell, it would break things and tonight he'd realized that she was careful with her money. He respected that. Matt was sleeping on a couch Maggie had in the middle of the room. Caleb was tired, but busy with Cassidy. They were trying on old boots and dancing around. Ryan was yawning while inching toward the door. Hmm, he always begged to stay up late. Right now, the kid wasn't making much sense.

Come to think of it, neither was Jared. It was almost midnight. He'd need to get up in just another five hours. Yet, when he looked at Maggie and noted her hands, small and delicate, he shook his head. "I'll put the tree in its stand. It will only take a minute if we all work together."

"We have church in the morning." Ryan sounded just like Grandpa Billy.

"See, I don't want to keep you any longer." Maggie moved toward the front door as if to open it.

"Got an aspirin?" Jared asked.

Maggie stopped. "You have a headache?"

"No, but we need to put an aspirin in the water along with the Christmas tree food you purchased."

She smiled, no longer looking tired, but back to looking mischievous. "Are you telling me the tree has a headache?"

Jared could see Ryan shaking his head.

"No, but I'm telling you I've had real Christmas trees all my life and know what to do. Now, shall my boys and I stay a few minutes longer or do you really want to do this on your own?"

"I really want to go to church in the morning," Cassidy decided to add to the conversation, never mind she was off topic. "I haven't been in a long time."

Ryan stopped shaking his head and Jared noted the deer-in-the-headlights expression on his son's face.

"No, not this time," Maggie said. "We have things to do and—"

"She can come with us," Caleb volunteered. "We drive right by your shop every Sunday morning."

It was on the tip of Jared's tongue to say he could pick up both of them, but if he were to appear at church with both Maggie and Cassidy in tow, he might as well put an *I real-*

ize she's single and cute and I'm interested sign on the back of his shirt.

He wasn't interested. But she was single and cute.

He wasn't looking for cute.

"We'd be glad to stop by and pick her up."

"Please, Mommy. I'll be good. I'll go to bed right now." Without waiting for an answer, Cassidy ran up the steps.

"Let's finish the tree," Maggie suggested softly. Jared noted that she hadn't given him a yes or no answer about Cassidy.

The minutes stretched into almost an hour until it was well after midnight when he finished. She'd tried—the whole time—to tell him it wasn't necessary, tried to convince him that either she could handle it herself or he could stop by tomorrow afternoon, but Jared had some thinking to do before church, during church and after church.

Some of it was about her and coming back tomorrow would only complicate matters.

His only son still awake was Ryan, and he was a glum participant in cleaning up the pine needles that had fallen to the floor. He didn't look overjoyed when Maggie said that Cassidy could come to church with them, either.

Jared picked up Matt to carry him to the truck and Maggie headed upstairs to find Caleb. Jared was just coming back in the door when she came down. Ryan met her at the bottom of the stairs and held out his arms. Maggie handed over Caleb. Ryan headed for the truck.

When had Ryan gotten so tall?

Once everyone was buckled in, Jared got behind the wheel and with a yawn, headed home. Ryan, sitting on the passenger side, didn't say a word. Unusual? No. But tonight, there was just a bit more determination in his silence.

"You got something on your mind?" Jared finally asked.

For a moment, Ryan didn't say anything, then in a rush, "You're sure spending a lot of time with them."

"Maggie and her daughter?"

"Yes."

"And this is bothering you?"

"Yes, I like it the way it is, with Billy and Uncle Joel. We don't need anybody else in our life."

"Anybody else meaning a woman?"

Again Ryan didn't answer.

"There's nothing for you to worry about," Jared said. "Maggie's helping me figure out some things with Caleb. I'm not interested in anything else right now."

Even in the darkened cab of the truck, Jared could see the disbelief on Ryan's face.

Instead of saying anything else, Jared focused his attention on the snowy road ahead because he didn't want to think about how *right now* had a bad habit of changing in the blink of an eye.

A light snow flaked the air Sunday morning. Maggie wished she'd have grabbed a warmer coat, but she just followed her daughter, who looked way too grown-up in her gray coat, blue velvet dress and black boots. Maggie garnered barely a wave as Cassidy exited the shop. That's how excited Cassidy was.

Maggie was of two minds as she watched her little girl, reddish-brown curls under a white winter hat, climb into Jared's truck. Jared helped her in before turning to wave at Maggie. He'd already offered to wait, had given her the chance to change her mind about coming with them, but no, this time Cassidy would have the front all to herself.

No, she wouldn't. Already Caleb, obviously ignoring his dad, was climbing in the front.

And Jared was moving him to the back where his car seat was.

Cassidy didn't need a car seat any longer. She was growing up, needing Maggie's guidance less and less, making good decisions, like *wanting to go to church*.

Maggie hoped that she, too, was making good decisions, like *letting Cassidy go to church*.

On one hand, Cassidy had been asking to go to church, and Maggie did want her daughter to know God. On the other hand, it opened a wound Maggie was trying to forget.

No, not trying to forget, a wound Maggie was trying to let heal.

Forget and forgive, two concepts Maggie seemed incapable of mastering. She'd never forget her late husband; she'd never forgive herself.

Heading back inside her shop, Maggie stopped before the Christmas tree. She'd promised Cassidy she wouldn't touch it. It hadn't looked so big back at Decker the Halls, but now it stood just to the left of her front entryway and looked huge, imposing, perfect. Ideas swirled. Christmas trees were really a shopkeeper's dream. There were so many products she could market. The tree was like a permanent salesman offering with outstretched boughs personal suggestions to anyone who walked through the door.

"Here, buy this soap. It smells like evergreen."

"Here, this hat is perfect for you. It will shelter your head."

"Here, try these socks. They'll keep your feet warm."

Maggie would carefully arrange the aged quilts right next to the new crochet blankets around the base. Doilies would be scattered like snowflakes. Scarves could be tied into bows and strategically placed.

Candy canes! Maggie needed candy canes!

Wanting to get started on those ideas practically made her fingers itch.

Heading upstairs, Maggie noted that a Sunday morning without Cassidy meant a different kind of silence than during the school week. The little apartment felt empty, wrong. Oh, evidence of her daughter was scattered across the room.

A pair of shoes tried on and discarded—Cassidy was her mother's daughter. Two books her daughter had pretended to read this morning. Pretended, because Cassidy didn't like books. Maggie loved them. A half-full glass of milk was on the kitchen table. "It didn't taste good," Cassidy had said. Since she said it every time Maggie gave her milk, Maggie no longer listened. The glass went back into the fridge for later, and now Cassidy would have to drink double.

Leisurely, Maggie cleaned the apartment, taking extra care and even moving the couch to vacuum. The only thing she did in their bedroom was change the sheets. It was about time to remind Cassidy that any toys left on the floor might disappear, especially since Cassidy's bedroom was also Maggie's bedroom and Maggie didn't like stepping on tiny things.

Chores finished, Maggie went on to other items on her list, namely making sure her shop was ready for tomorrow's crowd.

Wouldn't it be wonderful if she had record sales just in time for Christmas? Only three presents were under the tree: the red boots, a book and a movie. The phone rang just as Maggie finished wrapping an empty box for under the Christmas tree downstairs. Checking the Caller ID, Maggie sighed and picked up the receiver.

"Hello, Kelly."

"I need to know when you'll be arriving. I'll arrange for someone to pick you up from the airport." If one were to look up *stubborn* in the dictionary, Dan's mother's photo was there. Kelly Tate was nearing sixty. She was a retired professor and used to handing out assignments and expecting their criteria to be met.

"We're not coming for Christmas." Maggie tried for patience, but it was the fourth time they'd had this conversation. "We came for Thanksgiving. I can't afford the travel and I don't want to close the shop. I'll make last-minute sales on Christmas Eve."

"Consider the airline tickets my present to you."

"It's just not possible this Christmas, Kelly. There's a lot of work to be done around the shop. I'm building a business."

Kelly Tate was silent. Maggie knew the woman was gripping the phone and trying to thinking of something to say that would assure a Christmas spent with her granddaughter. Finally, she mustered, "Why couldn't you have opened a shop here? I'd have helped with the finances."

She would have, too. Then, she would have pitched in— make that *tried to take over*—with raising Cassidy, and sending Cassidy to expensive private schools, and to join every dance class, karate class and soccer team that Cassidy merely indicated she was interested in. She'd have offered to pick out Cassidy's clothes and frowned at what Maggie served at the dinner table.

Control. She would have interfered with the control that Maggie so desperately needed to feel when it came to managing her life and Cassidy's life.

So far, Kelly was unaware that Cassidy had any trouble with focus. Anything her grandchild did was just fine. And, if she knew how careful Maggie was with food choices and structure, she'd have criticized.

"Are you still there?" Kelly finally asked.

"I do appreciate the offer," Maggie said, "but Cassidy and I have things to do. Maybe next Christmas."

"And then you won't come Thanksgiving."

Kelly was good, always one step ahead, and she was correct. Maggie also knew that Cassidy was an only grandchild and Maggie knew how precious family was, but sometimes her mother-in-law was like a steamroller.

When Dan was alive, they'd visited when they could, never staying more than a week. Dan admitted he'd joined the military to get away from his mom.

"You can always come here." Maggie felt safe making the offer. Kelly had clubs and commitments and a small town in

Iowa just didn't offer the nightlife she was used to. Plus, there was no room at Maggie's little apartment and Kelly would go nuts stuck in one of the tiny rooms of the Roanoke Inn.

"May I speak with Cassidy?"

"She's at church."

"And you're not."

When Maggie didn't answer, Kelly backtracked. "I didn't mean for that to sound quite like it did. It's just, I'm glad she's at church. Did she go with a friend?"

"Yes."

"Did they invite you?"

"Yes."

"Oh, why don't you reconsider—"

"Kelly, Cassidy's going to be home real soon and we have an errand to run. I'll have her call you early this evening."

"All right. And remember, I'm praying for you."

After Kelly hung up, Maggie held the phone so tightly it hurt. Funny how those four little words *I'm praying for you* could pack such a punch. They erased every word Kelly spoke before and managed to end the conversation with an *I care about you* tone.

"You care about me because I'm raising your granddaughter," Maggie muttered, pushing away the unwanted feeling she got every year around Christmas—a feeling that Dan and Cassidy had spread a blanket over until Maggie knew the warmth of a family's steady embrace. Unfortunately, Dan's deployments had worn the blanket thin in a few places. His death had unraveled many a thread.

Cassidy, however, was a master at mending the torn and tattered pieces of Maggie's heart.

Yet, Maggie couldn't completely shed the memory of feeling unwanted.

Sunday school had been easy. Jared simply dropped off Cassidy at the same classroom as Matt. He wasn't too happy about the fact that it looked like they had arrived together. Caleb had surprised Jared, though. Instead of begging to stay with Cassidy, Caleb had walked into his kindergarten class as big as could be. Of course, Beth was the teacher and Caleb would get to tell about bringing Cassidy, provided Joel hadn't already texted his fiancée.

Afterward, instead of looking for Beth, Cassidy sat next to Jared. She swung her feet, up and down, and asked him, "Do you like my shoes?"

Not once, in all his years of being a father, had one of his children asked him if he liked their shoes. Cassidy's shoes were black with silver buckles.

"They're nice."

"I like your shoes," Caleb said.

Cassidy beamed at him.

"Hey, look who's visiting."

Finally, Beth joined them. Jared expected Cassidy to change where she was sitting, but she didn't. If anything, she scooted closer as if Beth and Joel needed room. Caleb scooted closer, too. Matt scowled. Ryan was sitting with one of his friends.

"My mom said I could come."

"Next time," Beth said, "we'll get her to come, too."

"That would be fun," Cassidy agreed.

A loud "Ahem" into the microphone got everyone's attention. Soon, Cassidy and Caleb were singing. Well, Caleb was doing something like singing. He didn't know the words, just the tune. Every once in a while Cassidy glanced up at Jared as if looking for approval. He nodded and that seemed to make her happy.

Before he knew it, the singing ended, the offering took just a few minutes and then Children's Bible Hour was called. Caleb quite happily took Cassidy by the hand and tugged her to the aisle.

Matt gave a look of terror. Children's Bible Hour was

for children three to eight. Matt was seven and had stopped going. He was straddling the fence between wanting to be like Ryan but also wanting to have fun. Clearly, he expected his dad to force him just to keep Cassidy happy.

But Cassidy didn't seem to notice. She let Caleb lead her along. Jared shrugged and Matt relaxed. In the moments before the sermon, Beth and Joel scooted down. Jared leaned over and whispered, "How does Cassidy know all the words to the songs?"

"Maggie sings all the time," Beth whispered back.

"Church songs?"

"They used to go to church before they moved here," Beth said softly. "Something happened right about the time her husband died. I'm not sure what, but I think Maggie is afraid of God now."

"Afraid of God?" Jared had stopped attending church after Mandy had died. He'd not been afraid of God. He'd been mad at God, furious, and glad to have somewhere to place his anger.

Make that misplace his anger.

Maggie'd said she saw no need for God. He'd interpreted that as a hole needing to be filled.

But afraid of God? Jared didn't know what to do with that information, but it sure made him want to help Maggie out.

Chapter Nine

The Totwell place was a farm so old that the once-white paint was now speckled gray. A living room window had boards nailed across it. Even to Maggie's untrained eye, it was easy to see that this was not an established *farm,* yet. There were chickens, some loose, and a barn that looked slightly better than the house.

"The Totwells have good ideas," Beth said, "but their money hasn't caught up to their ideas and they've probably bit off more than they can chew for beginners."

Sophia Totwell stepped out onto the porch. Two children quickly followed. In a heartbeat, Cassidy took off with her friend Lisa, from school, sliding across the snowy ground and heading for worlds unknown, namely the barn and all its animals. The little boy toddled behind. After a moment, everyone could hear Cassidy's squeal of joy.

Sophia shook her head. "They'll upset the chickens."

"I didn't know you could upset chickens," Maggie said.

"Neither did I," Sophia confided, "until we bought the farm."

"Let me go get her," Maggie said. "She doesn't need to scream."

"No, they'll be fine, and the kids are excited. We're so

far away from everyone that playmates are few and far between. Lisa's been excited since we got home from church. She even cleaned her room. I'd rather have a clean room than calm chickens any day."

When the laughter finally ended, Beth looked toward the barn. "You do know," she asked Maggie, "that your daughter asked Santa for a pair of red boots, a puppy, a baby brother and a horse?"

"A horse! When did that get added?" Maggie shook her head. "I haven't even taken her to see Santa. I've been waiting for the perfect time to coach her."

"Coach her?" Sophia asked.

"Yes, I want to coach her to ask Santa for a few things that actually might appear under the tree. So far, the only thing she's getting from that list is the red boots."

"Santa came to the school on Friday," Beth said. "I was his helper for a while. Quite a few kids asked for horses."

Sophia led them into the house. "Lisa's got all four—red boots, a puppy or two, a baby brother and a horse. She'd rather move back to Omaha or at least live in town and have playmates."

"Living in town doesn't necessarily mean playmates," Maggie said. "We live above the shop, not in a neighborhood, so there are no kids. Plus, we don't have a yard so she can't even invite friends over, not really. If I sat on Santa's knee, I'd be asking for a yard."

"I'd be asking for the perfect wedding dress," Beth put in.

"I'd be asking for a husband who's not always tired," Sophia said. "Speaking of which…"

The man entering the room had to be Kyle Totwell. Maggie hadn't met him before, but he shyly put out his hand for her to shake and then turned to Beth. "You think Joel'd have some time this afternoon to come out and help me put in a window?"

In answer, Beth whipped out her cell phone and sent a

text. A moment later she nodded. "He says give him about an hour."

Sounding ever so much like an old cowboy, he said, "Much obliged," before heading back outside.

All three women giggled, and Sophia said, "Sometimes I think he thinks he's John Wayne."

It was enough to change the mood back to humor. Sophia started them on a tour, which began in the living room where the boarded-up window was.

"When we got home from church last Sunday, someone had broken the window, climbed in and taken the presents under the tree," Sophia said.

"Did they take anything else?" Beth asked.

Maggie followed Sophia's eyes as they swept the room.

"We didn't notice anything else missing," Sophia said, "and quite honestly, if I were the thief, I'd take one look around my house and think to myself 'I'm not going to waste my time.'"

"Your house isn't a waste of time," Maggie said. "It fits you and only you."

"True," Sophia agreed. "The couch belonged to my grandmother, the kitchen table, too. All the utensils in my kitchen came from my mother and Kyle's. Even the quilt on our bed came from Grandma. Right now we live in a family cast-off melting pot of furniture and appliances."

"I didn't know my grandparents," Beth said. "I think you're lucky."

"I didn't know mine, either," Maggie added. "But I have a mother-in-law who takes up a lot of my time."

Both Sophia and Beth looked curious but neither ventured to ask. Maggie was glad. She didn't want to explain or complain about Kelly.

Sophia rubbed her hand on an old oak display cabinet. "This was Kyle's grandfather's. It's my favorite. We have antiques, but most are not in perfect condition like this one. Plus, they're not that easy to steal."

"Did they get all the kids' Christmas presents?" Maggie asked.

"No, I still have some hidden away to wrap but they got most."

"There's been a rash of break-ins," Beth said. "I know of at least four other families." For the next few minutes, they discussed the whens and wheres of the thefts. Seemed they only happened on Sunday morning while people were at church but didn't seem to be in a concentrated area.

Another reason for me not to go to church, Maggie thought but didn't say.

"Come see the rest of the house," Sophia finally said. "It will be cute when we finish. I'll tell you how we got here, too."

The farmhouse had two stories. Downstairs was a living room and kitchen and bath. Upstairs were two bedrooms and a bath. Sophia led them to a bedroom that was smaller than the one Maggie shared with her daughter. About an hour later, Maggie knew that Kyle Totwell had been close to his grandfather who'd been an Iowa farmer in the fifties. That farm was long gone and Kyle's dad worked in Omaha, as far away from the farm as he could be, but Kyle had a dream and right now, the Totwells, albeit haltingly, were living that dream.

"Kyle didn't realize how hard farming really is," Sylvia confided.

Maggie remembered Jared saying something about buying too many cows too soon, but she didn't quite understand why that was a bad thing. Maybe it was a money thing.

"The previous owners, who've been gone forever, left a few things in the barn and down in the basement. I'm just now getting around to sorting through everything in the attic. That's why I called you. We thought it was pretty much empty except for rotting furniture, but then we moved an old bed frame and found the trunks.

In anticipation of their visit, Kyle had carried the trunks into their bedroom and Sophia had started to spread out the clothes. Because the room was small, she'd quickly consumed the space. Some items were rotted beyond repair, others were a yellow that Maggie couldn't begin to tackle, but a few had promise.

"The ugliest trunk actually had the nicest clothes," Sylvia said. "But, it smelled of mothballs."

"Mothballs? Now there's a smell I haven't missed," Beth said.

Maggie went down to her knees by the first trunk. Sophia had half unpacked it. A quick look through what was left told Maggie everything she needed to know. "Mostly ladies' clothes from after the 1950s."

"How can you tell?" Sophia asked.

"By where the zippers are and the style." Maggie pulled a skirt from under a jacket. "Whoever owned these was very slim, probably a size four."

"I can't see a farmer's wife wearing that skirt," Sophia said.

Maggie nodded, her throat tightening a bit. She wasn't a size four, but this skirt was very much like the red velvet one she'd worn two Fridays ago when she'd paid Beth a visit at school. Not practical, but very stylish. And not the usual style of a farmer's wife. Probably not what Jared's wife would have worn to see her boys' teacher and certainly not to chase after her boys.

"Who says?" Beth challenged. "I think fifty years ago, maybe you were right, but today, a farmer's wife can wear anything she pleases."

"I wouldn't wear that skirt even if I was a size four. I'm happy in jeans," Sophia said.

"She wore jeans to church this morning," Beth told Maggie.

Sophia snapped, "It's the going to church that's important, not what you wear."

"Touché," Beth replied.

Twice Maggie went out to check on Cassidy. Both times Cassidy said this was the best day ever and the only thing that would possibly make it better was if she could take one of the horses home with her.

Sophia poured iced tea and brought cookies to the ladies as they went through the clothes. One pile was throwaways. One pile was giveaways. The last pile was Maggie's takeaways. Sophia gladly took the fifty dollars offered.

"But we didn't find a wedding dress," Beth said sadly.

"What kind of wedding dress do you want?" Sophia asked.

"We decided to go vintage." Ever the teacher, with her fingers Beth drew in the air. "Joel's wearing a turn-of-the-century black suit with bow tie and spats. I've even convinced him to wear a ruffled, maroon-front shirt."

"It's called a 'gambler' look," Maggie told Sophia.

"What are spats?"

"They go on the shoes," Maggie explained. "Have you ever seen a marching band? It's the material that covers the instep and ankle."

"Oh, I know what you're talking about. Why would you want him to wear spats?"

"I'm having the wedding of my dreams. After all, you only get married once."

Sophia nodded.

Maggie wanted to nod, wanted to agree, but she knew it wasn't always true. She was just twenty-seven and if she were to only be married once, her dreams for a bigger family, for someone to welcome home—a home with a yard and a puppy—at night, go for walks with, okay, *cuddle with,* were over. Instead she asked, "Have you convinced Jared to wear the spats?"

"No, not yet. I'm still working on him. I want everything to be authentic."

"So," Sophia said softly, "you want a turn-of-the-century wedding dress."

"Yes, but so far, we haven't found the right one."

"What size are you?"

Beth looked a bit surprised but wasn't shy. "I'm a twelve."

"I'm a ten, but it might work," Sophia said. "Follow me."

Back downstairs they went, to a storage area under the stairs. Sophia knew right where to look. After a minute of re-arranging, grunting and a few interesting words like, "Well, shoot a monkey," she got hold of a good-sized cardboard box and dragged it into the living room. If Sophia weren't so far away, Maggie'd think about hiring her for the shop. She'd done everything right. She'd chosen an acid-free box and then she'd actually taken the time to fold whatever was inside accordion style with tissue paper between each fold. There was crumpled tissue everywhere.

"Oh, my," Beth said as Sophia held up the wedding dress.

"It was my great-grandmother's. She got married in 1936. My grandmother wore it in 1958. Mom skipped it and bought a new one, but I wore it just ten years ago. I'm saving it for Lisa, if she wants it, but it's too beautiful not to share. Would you like to borrow it?"

Beth managed a nod. Maggie doubted she could manage even that. She wasn't breathing. In all her years, she'd never seen, come across, anything so beautiful. And, obviously the women who'd worn it before Sophia had cared enough to preserve it. Maggie went to her knees, holding the material reverently in her hands and gently spreading it so Beth could see its true potential. "Rayon satin, net lace, a lace overcoat."

"Will it fit me?" Beth asked. "It looks small."

"It's a bias gown," Maggie said. "It's meant to hug your figure. You'll look awesome."

"I'm a size bigger than Sophia so there's more to hug.

Are you sure?" Beth didn't look or sound near as excited as Maggie thought she should be.

"I'm sure, plus with the lace overcoat, you'll feel like a princess."

"You already look like one." A gust of cold air preceded Joel's entry. Immediately, Beth did look like a princess thanks to the expression on her face. Love did that to a gal. Maggie only hoped her face didn't look so much like an open book because right behind Joel came Jared, and Maggie's first instinct was to smile.

Jared shook the snow from his boots in the entryway. That's when he had noticed Maggie down on her hands and knees in the living room looking ever so much like a kid who'd just opened a much-wanted Christmas package.

"You going to stay here in the cold or go in?" Joel asked, tugging Jared forward. It was love, pure and simple, that had his little brother in a rush. Like a moth to a flame, Joel crossed the room to put his arm around Beth.

Kyle helped his wife to her feet, but Jared could tell that Maggie was happy right where she was.

"What do you have that out for?" Kyle looked at the wedding dress in Maggie's hands. "You buying it, too?"

Sophia almost let go of his hand and fell to the floor. "Are you kidding? No, I'd never sell it. But, I'm going to lend it to Beth for her wedding."

Jared studied the dress Maggie was holding and opened his mouth to say, "Looks small." The slightest shake of Maggie's chin told him that she knew what he was thinking and that she thought he should think twice.

Good advice.

Joel didn't need such assistance. "It will look great on you."

Yep, Joel wasn't just in love, he was besotted. Otherwise, he'd never have agreed to wear spats at his wedding.

Kyle was no dummy. He was helping his wife to her feet again and whispering something in her ear that had her smiling.

"How long have you two been married?" Joel asked.

"Going on ten years."

Jared closed his eyes. That's how long he'd been married. He opened his eyes and saw Maggie Tate watching him, an expression he couldn't read on her face.

"We got married in Omaha," Sophia said, "at a castle."

"A castle?" Beth was clearly intrigued. She, however, looked at Joel and said, "Don't worry. I'm quite happy that we'll be getting married at your place."

"No castles in Roanoke," Jared said.

"I'm surprised there's a castle in Omaha," Joel said. "I hear there's a shortage of moats there."

"It was built by a newspaper tycoon," Sophia said, "and it really looks like a castle." She practically flew from the room and after a moment returned with a white frilly photograph album. "See, turrets and everything."

Maggie gently lay the wedding dress back in its box and got to her feet. Looking at the pictures, the women oohed and aahed. Even Joel, peering over Beth's shoulder, looked vaguely interested. Kyle stood back aways. His face had that slightly embarrassed but proud look a man gets when his wife or kids have put him in an unwanted but favorable limelight.

Jared came a little farther in the room, not liking the cold against his back—a draft came through the broken window—and wanting to see the castle and feel a part of the conversation, even if it was about weddings. "Quincy didn't build a castle when he started the *Roanoke Times*."

"Hard to build much more than a shed with a once-a-month tabloid," Joel agreed. The brothers were the only Roanoke natives in the room.

"I had six bridesmaids," Sophia remembered.

"I'm just having my sisters. And Maggie's making their dresses. They'll be the same burgundy—"

"Dark maroon," Maggie corrected.

"—as the shirts Joel and Jared will be wearing."

"Cool," Sophia said approvingly. "I had pink, and I carried roses. Then the cake had roses—at least the first cake—on it. My cake was a five tier, and we ran out. My father ran to the nearest store and bought a big sheet cake. Otherwise, we wouldn't have had a piece to put in the fridge for our first anniversary."

"'Bout ran out of that one, too," Kyle contributed. "I thought her dad was going to faint."

Sophia chuckled. "Dad was more stressed by the wedding than either my mother or me. He found the place and he was actually more of a wedding planner than our actual wedding planner. I kept trying to calm him down and tell him the only thing he had to do was give me away."

"We're getting married in Joel's living room," Beth said. "Billy's giving me away."

It's my living room, Jared thought to himself. Immediately, he blocked the thought. It was Joel's home, too, and Billy's job was to give the bride away. Their stepfather had been honored when they had asked.

Beth was still speaking. "I won't need to decorate much because we're doing a Christmasy theme. The tree will still be up and there's a bunch of empty presents I've wrapped that will be placed around the room."

"Where did you get married, Maggie?" Sophia closed her album.

"I got married in Hawaii."

The oohs and aahs came again, but Maggie merely shook her head. "Dan was about to be deployed, and we didn't have much time, so we went to the courthouse and the Justice of the Peace married us."

"No bridesmaids," Sophia said.

"No cake," Beth added.

"No hassle," Joel said, earning him a punch.

Jared tried to imagine what Maggie must have looked like, what? Eight or nine years ago? Judging by her looks, she'd have just been barely twenty, only a little older than Mandy.

"You didn't want all the fuss?" he asked. "I mean, you like clothes so much."

"Clothes are easy—weddings are not."

Jared wondered what Maggie meant by *weddings are not*. Was it just the actual wedding day? Or, had she been thinking clothes are easy, and the wedding day and all the days after, the married days that followed, were not.

Chapter Ten

It took almost an hour for the men to replace the glass in the Totwells' living room window. The room went from cold, thanks to no glass in the frame, to freezing thanks to no glass in the frame *and* kids opening and closing the front door every two minutes. Cassidy was in her element, with everyone she loved nearby and lots of kids to play with. The yard, puppies and horses were just icing on the cake.

Finally, when it looked like one more door slam would send the men into anti-Santa mode, Beth headed outside to play with them. That's what the kids really wanted, an adult to play with them.

Maggie watched the men for a few minutes. "I might need to do this. The windows in my apartment are in wooden frames like this. I know I have some mold."

"We're grateful to be switching to double paned," said Kyle.

Maggie nodded. She'd be grateful, too. Maybe in a year or two. Leaving the men to their work, she sat next to Sophia and inch by inch they went over the dress. It was in great condition, considering its age, but the net lace needed stabilizing. Maggie could do that. There was also a bit of dirt along the hemline.

"Do you think this is the dress Beth really wants?" Sophia asked. "She acted excited for a moment and then nothing."

"She's overwhelmed. And, if it's not the dress for her, I can still do the repairs for you since you're thinking ahead to Lisa. I'll take it to the store and put it on one of my dress forms. Believe me, when she sees it, she'll fall over with joy."

"That would be great. I sew, quite a bit, but this is out of my league. Mom hired someone to go over it before my wedding."

"They did a pretty decent job." Not as good as Maggie would have done. She could tell repairs done by commission compared to repairs done by commitment. For her, working on a dress like this would be a labor of love.

"Mom wanted everything to be perfect."

"Will you and Kyle head to Omaha for Christmas?" Maggie asked, starting to carefully return the dress to the box.

"Yes, both sets of parents are there. We'll do Kyle's house in the morning, and mine in the afternoon. I'm not sure how we'll manage everything. Both sides are big gift givers. We spend the night, but Kyle wants an early start for home the day after Christmas. We can't leave the cows alone, and there's really no one else to pitch in."

"Did you ask Joel or Jared?"

"Joel's getting married just a week after Christmas," Sophia reminded. "And, Jared… Well, Kyle doesn't feel comfortable asking him. He's already so busy."

Maggie looked over to where Jared was doing something with a paintbrush near the window frame. He did look more serious than the other two men.

That serious look might make someone think twice about approaching him. Two weeks ago, Maggie would have thought the same thing, considered Jared McCreedy daunting, but now, not so much. If anything, it was just that he was so straightforward in everything he did. Standing around talking future wedding plans hadn't been something he *wanted* to do, but he'd done it and even asked a question or two. She thought back to their talk Friday night in the church nursery. For all his rough exterior, Jared actually just might have a true father's heart.

"Where are you going for Christmas?" Sophia asked.

"I'm looking forward to just staying home. We went to New York and my mother-in-law's for Thanksgiving. It was a whirlwind of activity. I'm ready for some downtime. Cassidy and I will eat, build a snowman, eat again and then watch a favorite Christmas movie."

"That actually sounds like fun." Sophia looked at the Christmas tree standing in the corner of her living room.

Maggie looked, too. She watched as the three men neared the end of installing the window. Once they'd started, Jared had relaxed. She admired how easily he worked as a team and followed Joel's instructions.

"We have to pack to go to Omaha," Sophia said. "Both sides of the family celebrate big. Then, coming back, we'll be bringing more stuff. Sometimes I don't know what to do with it all."

Kelly didn't quite get the concept of too much stuff. If she had her way, Maggie's apartment would be so crowded, there'd be no room to walk.

That was just one more reason why Maggie and Cassidy were taking care of themselves this Christmas.

The men finished about the time the children and Beth came in. Matt walked right next to her, talking more than Maggie had seen before. He had an earnest expression—quite like his dad's—on his face. Cassidy and Lisa were just behind, all red cheeked and laughing. Caleb and Lisa's little brother, David, skipped along behind them. They'd taken off their boots in the entryway, but Caleb's wet socks left soppy footprints across the room. David made it worse by purposely stepping wherever Caleb stepped.

"Where's Ryan?" Jared asked.

Lisa stopped, looking around. "Still in the barn, I think. He doesn't want to come in. We told him he had to but he laughed."

Jared shook his head.

"Where did you get married, Jared?" Maggie asked, taking them back to the earlier conversation. "Everyone else shared."

The paintbrush he held in his hand stilled. Joel almost seemed to settle back, as if anticipating the response.

Maggie wished the words back. It really hadn't been her place to ask.

He looked at Joel, a slow grin with a half smirk, spreading across his face. "I got married at the church, like my dad before me and his dad before him."

"I should have guessed the church," Maggie said.

"I never would have guessed you for a Justice-of-the-Peace kind of gal." He nodded at the wedding gown. "You're so talented and creative. Seems you would have put together quite a show."

Maggie shook her head. "My dad was in North Korea and couldn't get back. Dan's mother told him not to get married. Then, she didn't come to the wedding because she thought if she refused, we wouldn't get married. By the time she realized we were serious, it was too late. We were married and she'd missed it."

"Why didn't she want you to get married?" Sophia was clearly puzzled.

"It wasn't that she didn't want us to get married, but more she wanted us to get married in New York so that she could plan it."

"What's wrong with that?"

"I didn't want a big wedding and neither did Dan. We just wanted to get married and get busy with life, have some fun, start a family. She wouldn't listen when he tried to tell her."

"What about your mother?" Beth asked. "You never talk about her. Did she come?"

Maggie stood up and busied herself putting away the wedding dress. She made sure each fold was protected with tissue paper. She wasn't going to cry, not with all these people around, not with Jared around.

"I haven't seen my mother since I was twelve. I have no idea where she is."

Sophia put a hand on Maggie's arm, staying Maggie's movements. "That's rough. I'm so sorry."

"It's life," Maggie said simply. "You deal with it, and go on. All you can do is make sure you don't make the same mistakes with your own children."

"Mothers make mistakes," Beth said gently.

Both McCreedy men were nodding. Joel was probably thinking about Beth's mother, who was currently serving time for embezzlement after trying to frame him. Jared was probably thinking of Mandy who wasn't around to help him raise three boys.

Not her mistake really, Maggie thought. Unlike Maggie's mother, Mandy McCreedy's leaving hadn't been desired, planned and executed by a woman who *chose* to leave behind a child.

Driving straight to church from the Totwells', Jared looked in the rearview window at his sons. Caleb was in the middle, happy as could be. He'd eaten two hot dogs—lately everybody seemed inclined to serve hot dogs—and had two of Matt's toy men and was doing battle. Matt was happy, too. He'd spent the entire dinnertime telling Beth everything he wanted for Christmas—skateboard, bike, scooter with sparks, etc.—and was now dreaming about getting them all.

Not a chance.

Ryan was the quiet one. He'd eaten half a hot dog.

Joel's eyes met Jared's.

So Joel saw it, too.

The church's parking lot was full. The Christmas season made people seek out hearth and home. There was no better hearth and home than church. Jared stopped in front of the door and let out the boys. No sense having them tramp through the snow and take more of it inside than necessary.

"You see Billy's car?" Joel asked.

"No, but I haven't looked yet. Ryan, you guys find Billy or go to our usual place and sit down. I'll be right behind."

"Yeah, Dad."

Jared expected Joel to exit but he didn't. The minute Ryan shut the door, Joel asked, "What's with Ryan?"

Jared thought about pretending ignorance but the truth always came out in the end. "He thinks I'm spending too much time with Maggie. He told me last night that he likes the way it is right now with just me and Billy taking care of them."

Joel whistled. "I didn't see that coming."

Jared pulled forward. Another car was behind him wanting to deposit people at the front entrance.

"Me, either. Especially since there's nothing between Maggie and me outside of having kids the same age."

"Are you sure about that?"

Jared nodded as he pulled into a parking spot. "If, and I do mean if, I date or get married again, I want someone who'll be happy as a farmer's wife. I don't see Maggie taking to that role. She likes fancy clothes and running her shop."

"You've spent the whole weekend tog—" Joel began.

"We happened to be at the same places at the same time. Saturday was Beth's fault."

"I hear you had a good time."

Jared opened the door and stepped into the snow. "I did have a good time. It's time I start getting out more."

Joel put his hands together as if in prayer. "About time. Please keep going out. And you couldn't find a nicer girl than Maggie."

"Who doesn't believe in God," Jared pointed out. "When you invited her to join us tonight, she didn't even hesitate in saying no."

"She believes in God," Joel said. "Beth and I think something happened when her husband died and that she's not been able to shake it."

Joel shut the truck's passenger side door and came around to join Jared. Putting one gloved hand on Jared's shoulder, he said, "I saw that happen to somebody else I know."

Jared made the phone call Monday morning. Monday before noon, he picked up Caleb from school and they went to Dr. Lazurus's office. Lazurus looked well past retirement, acted as if he knew everything—he did—and had the energy of someone just out of med school. He'd delivered all three of Jared's boys as well as Jared.

The front desk staff greeted Caleb by name and promised, "No shots." The nurse, who'd been in Jared's graduating class, weighed and measured Caleb, also promising, "No shots."

"Thanks, Patty. When did you move back?"

The Maynards were another farm family that had been around forever.

Patty chuckled. "Four months ago. I've been at church every time you have. I finished my degree and worked in an emergency room for six years, and finally realized why I wasn't happy."

"Why?"

"I missed my family, and I didn't like living where I could spit out the window and hit the house next door."

Jared grinned. She'd grown up with five brothers and could out-spit just about all of them.

Finally Jared and Caleb were sent to a room to wait for Dr. Lazurus. Once in the tiny observation room, Jared was at a loss. There were a few magazines, none interested Caleb.

There were a few toys, all too young for Caleb, or maybe Caleb had already played with them when Billy brought him to the doctor's.

Caleb did exactly what he did at home. He explored, first everything on counters and then he lay on the floor and crawled under the table to see if anything was hidden under there. He went to the bathroom, again. He wandered out into the hall to watch the fish. Then, he wanted to wrestle.

"Not here, Caleb," Jared said.

"Why not?"

"This is a place of business."

Caleb looked around as if not convinced. Idly he stuck out his foot and kicked Jared gently in the shins and then grinned.

At home, Jared would have sent Caleb to his room, and if Caleb balked, Jared would have escorted him. Here at a doctor's office, Jared didn't have the same options, not unless he wanted the doctor to see a screaming kid when he finally showed up.

"Stop."

Caleb did, sort of. He stood by the door and kicked it instead of Jared.

Jared was in the process of pulling Caleb back to the bench to sit beside him when the door opened and Dr. Lazurus came in.

"Good to see you, Jared. Billy feeling all right?"

It was an innocent question but reminded Jared of who usually brought Caleb to the doctor, and who—now that Jared thought about it—usually made sure that a few toys and a drawing table came along.

"He's fine. I brought Caleb because I have a few questions."

Dr. Lazurus consulted a folder and then wrote something down before patting the observation table. Caleb climbed up easily. It took all of three minutes. Dr. Lazurus checked

Caleb's ears, both with an instrument and then in a room with a machine. Jared didn't get to go to that test. Then, Dr. Lazurus did an eye test and listened to Caleb chatter about who got a gold star in class this morning. He also checked Caleb's reflexes and listened to Caleb talk about how many toys he had before checking Caleb's heart and listening to Caleb talk about having hot dogs last night at the Totwells'. Dr. Lazurus had patience. Checking the heart was a problem because Caleb needed to be quiet, and Caleb wasn't done telling Dr. Lazurus who was at dinner last night.

A few minutes later, Jared sat in Dr. Lazurus's office. It was full of toys and photos of his patients. Jared had no clue where his photo was in the collage, but he knew it was there. Caleb's was near the door.

Nothing wrong with Caleb's smile. Caleb could give half of it to Matt and no one would notice.

Jared suddenly wished he'd come to every single doctor's appointment with all his boys. He needed to know how they acted and what the doctor said firsthand. He needed to be involved in every facet.

Because Mandy wasn't here, and Billy was slowing down.

And because it was a father's job.

Maggie Tate had probably been to every appointment.

Caleb was up front with a nurse who also happened to have been his cradle roll teacher at church. Dr. Lazurus studied a chart before saying, "Caleb's teacher has good instincts. I'm glad we're looking into this now."

"I'm hoping it's just that he's an active little boy," Jared said. "I've been watching him all week at home, though. He runs roughshod over Matt, who takes it pretty well. He tries the same with Ryan. My older son's a little too willing to barricade himself in his bedroom."

Dr. Lazurus nodded.

"I've ordered a few books off the internet," Jared continued. "Maggie Tate recommended them."

"She's a good resource," Dr. Lazurus agreed. "Every child is different, though. What's working for Maggie might not work for Caleb."

"What happens if we wait until first grade, see how much he matures in a year? If we're having the same problems, I'll take action."

"It's an option," Dr. Lazurus agreed. "If you're right, nothing lost. However, if you're wrong, and Caleb does have Attention Deficit, then you've lost a whole year where he could have been getting help."

"What kind of help?"

"Some of it's diet."

Maggie had mentioned limiting sugar, watching dyes and something about fried chicken.

"I can work on his diet," Jared volunteered. "He gets way too much sugar."

"Some of it has to do with learning styles and getting him additional outside-the-classroom help—help that the state pays for."

"I can pay for what my son needs."

"It has nothing to do with what parents can and cannot pay. It has everything to do with the resources the school district is required by law to provide."

"I don't want him to be different."

"Every child is different. It would be boring if we were all the same."

Jared tried to smile. "That's one thing Caleb isn't. That kid's never boring."

Dr. Lazurus put the file on his desk and waited.

"Can you do the testing here?" Jared finally said.

"Some. Based on what you've told me and what his teachers say, I'd like you to see a pediatric allergist along with the developmental pediatrician. You'll need to go into Des Moines. Has the school already made a recommendation?"

"So, it could it be something besides Attention Deficit?"

"It could."

Dr. Lazurus's eyes were the same color as Maggie's, a dark liquid green. Both were wise when it came to children. Wiser than Jared, that's for sure.

Jared left the doctor, went to the front where the receptionist handed him two business cards for some center in Des Moines and the allergy place. She also gave him a sheet of paper, some sort of behavioral list for Caleb's teacher, as well as the paperwork for Caleb's blood tests.

Blood tests?

"They'll be asking for these," the nurse said. "You might as well be prepared."

Somewhat in a daze, Jared guided his son to the truck. Suddenly, this whole focus issue seemed more than Jared expected.

Unaware of his dad's turmoil, Caleb opened his lunch box and took out his peanut butter and jelly sandwich. "You want half, Dad?"

"No, I'm good."

"You're always good."

Not always, Jared thought, turning on the ignition and heading back toward the elementary school. Ryan had play rehearsal right after school, and Jared had promised to help with the sets.

I'm not good at always making the right choices when it comes to my boys. That had been Mandy's job, with Jared sharing his thoughts. Making all these decisions alone was hard. But it had to be done. Jared thanked God for the doctor, for everyone trying to help, especially Maggie, and for the cold slapping against his cheeks.

What was it Maggie had said last Friday night while they were in the nursery?

This is nothing. It could be so much worse.

Maggie's words of wisdom played over and over in his mind. She was right that it could be worse. Still, Jared couldn't grasp the concept of this being *nothing*. It was something. Something Jared didn't know how to deal with.

One more thing Jared didn't know how to deal with.

Chapter Eleven

Maggie stood on the stage of Roanoke Elementary and watched as the children who'd won the coveted lead roles practiced. Ryan McCreedy, without his handheld, was actually a pretty animated kid. Cassidy had been of two minds about trying out. She thought it would be great fun to be on stage but a great amount of work to memorize her lines.

In the end, Cassidy had won the role of lead elf, which is how Maggie wound up making fifty elf hats. Cassidy had no lines but got to stay by the giant Santa bag and hand out presents to all the elves who then went into the audience and distributed them randomly.

Each present contained a candy cane.

"We really appreciate you helping out with the costumes," Cassidy's teacher said. Mrs. Youst was older, almost retirement age, and had been teaching second grade longer than Maggie had been alive. She had the patience of Job.

"I like to help."

"Used to be all the mothers knew how to sew. Now, there's just a handful. You're the best thing to come along since Mandy McCreedy."

Maggie bristled about being compared to Mandy. From

what everyone was saying, Maggie knew she was about as different from Mandy as different could be.

"My job is sewing. Beth said she'd help." Maggie nodded toward Beth, who was in front of the four students playing the leads. She had a script in one hand. Her other hand was like a conductor, up and down, as she gave instructions.

Maggie studied the students. Ryan's Santa costume was finished. Good thing because he looked to be in a grumpy mood lately. Maggie wasn't quite sure why, but whenever she came near him, to adjust a seam or check on a hem, he practically tripped over himself to get away. Mrs. Santa was a little lost in her costume. The pillow needed to be adjusted. The two Claus children were fine.

Glued to Beth's side was Matt. He wasn't a lead character, but an elf. Still, he liked to be where Beth was.

Caleb had shown up after rehearsal started. He followed behind his dad, waved at everybody like they were waiting for him and even managed to drive in a nail or two. Jared was standing right beside him, guiding every move. It looked like Jared was guiding everyone's moves. He barked orders, looking stressed the whole time and didn't give even a little encouragement to the crew he directed.

Okay, Maggie could cut him some slack. The scenery should have been finished a week ago, but the other dad who'd volunteered had wound up working overtime, so Jared and a few others had taken over and were now behind.

Jared looked up at one point, found her staring and gave her a smile. Then, just as quickly, he went back to what he was doing, leaving Maggie to wonder what the smile meant.

"Nothing, it meant nothing," she muttered.

"What did you say?" Mrs. Youst asked.

"I didn't say anything," Maggie said. After all, if she didn't say anything, that meant she'd said nothing which is exactly what she'd said.

Maggie looked around for Cassidy and finally located

her inside the giant Santa sack that Maggie had finished just last week.

"There are no presents in there," Maggie shouted.

"I know!"

Comfortable that the costumes were fine, Maggie called Cassidy over, bundled her up and they started walking home. They'd not even crossed the street outside the school before Maggie realized everything wasn't fine. Cassidy's head was down. She seemed very interested in staring at exactly where her boots landed and how long they stayed in one spot before she stepped to another.

"You might as well tell me," Maggie encouraged.

"Well, I did throw Matt's lunch box today, but when the teacher asked me to stop, I did. Right away. And I even went and picked it up and gave it back to him."

"Why did you mess with his lunch box?"

"He had two candy bars. Two! I never even get one." Cassidy was very aware of the good things her friends got to eat that she didn't.

"Candy bars are treats, nothing more, and certainly nothing to throw a lunch box over."

"I told him I was sorry."

On one hand, Cassidy's teacher hadn't deemed it necessary to write a note. And, Cassidy had owned up to the misdeed. Granted, she thought that Maggie already knew.

Just another manic Monday.

"Anything else happen?" Maggie asked.

Her shoes still bore the lion's share of Cassidy's attention. "No," she squeaked.

Maggie knew something else had happened; she just wasn't sure what.

The walk home was quiet. Cassidy seemed determined to be good, as if being good now would remedy any past or future offenses.

As they neared Hand Me Ups, Maggie started walking

faster. Even a block away she could see the door open to her shop. No one was entering or exiting.

The door shouldn't be open.

Maggie had put up her Be Back At… sign before leaving for Cassidy's school. She'd locked the door, no doubt. And she was definitely back before her specified time.

"Stay here!" she ordered Cassidy.

Running had never been her strong point. Today, this moment, changed all that. She sludged through the snow, her boots sinking momentarily but never for long and finally skidded to a stop by her front door, looked in and almost went to her knees. The once-proud Christmas tree was leaning toward the cash register. There were doilies on its branches, but that was about it.

"Mama, what's wrong?" Cassidy hadn't been able to obey, and for once, Maggie didn't blame her.

"It's all right. It's all right." Maggie didn't know what else to say. Her repetitious words didn't begin to soothe Cassidy.

"It's all right." Maggie felt inside her purse and pulled out her phone. She punched in 911. Even as the connection began, Henry Throxmorton from across the street hurried toward her. His old-fashioned gray coat flapped in the wind. "I've already called the chief of police," he shouted. "He's on his way."

Maggie stared at Hand Me Ups's door, noting the screwdriver stuck in the lock and the snow blowing in on her clean floor. "Did you see what happened?"

"No, but my wife was upstairs in our apartment and thought she heard a car backfire. When she looked out, she saw your door was open." He took Maggie by the arm, his red face grim as he looked at her shop and then up and down the street. "Come to my place. You don't want to touch anything. We can watch your building until the police get here."

"I don't want to leave the door open." She wanted to go inside, start inventorying, start cleaning, start screaming, but she couldn't do that last one until Cassidy was asleep or something.

Henry kicked the door shut and took her arm again. He turned her toward his shop and gave a little push. Cassidy ran ahead of her.

"I didn't think anything of it," Henry said, "until Tess said something about your door being open and you not being there and maybe I should head over to close it. I'd seen you leave for the school play a good hour ago, so I knew something was wrong."

They were halfway across the street when Henry shared, "I've been broken into four times in the last ten years. Best to let the police go in first." Right there in the middle of the Main Street, he patted his head. Maggie imagined stitches and lumps.

"Mama, what's wrong?" Cassidy repeated.

"I think someone broke into our shop."

Think? She didn't think. She knew. She blinked back tears.

"Did they take my presents?" Cassidy's face turned white and she turned, taking three steps back the way they'd come. Maggie clutched her daughter close. There were only three presents under the tree, all for Cassidy.

"I'm not sure," Maggie said. "When the police come, we'll find out."

"Wait!" Cassidy said. "Did they take your money, Mama? Did they hurt your clothes?"

"I don't know about the money, but they didn't have time to hurt all the clothes. We'll be fine. The important thing is that we weren't home and so we're not hurt. God took care…"

She'd almost said *God took care of us.* But, at the moment, she didn't want to give God credit for that. Who knew what damage the half-fallen Christmas tree—a tree Maggie hadn't really wanted—had done. Most of the stuff underneath had been consignment. Maggie would now have to pay vendors for stock she'd collected nothing on.

And what about upstairs? Besides Cassidy's presents there wasn't much else, not that a crook would want, but the computer…

If they took the computer, she'd be dead in the water. All her records, her contacts… Yes, she had the important stuff saved to a flash drive, but her hard drive contained so much more.

"It's odd they struck today. You've never been gone this long on a Monday afternoon," Henry said.

"It's getting closer to the day of the program. I wanted to see if everything was all right."

"Did you tell anyone you were going to close up your shop?"

Maggie thought for a moment. "I don't think it's a matter of who I told, but more a matter of who saw me arrive at the school and would be able to figure out why I was there and how long I might be."

"So, any parent picking up his or her child would know why you were at the school."

Maggie nodded. "Every parent who paid attention."

But wouldn't those same parents also know that Maggie was living hand to mouth? And that the only item of value she had was a sweet-faced seven-year-old girl?

For the first time since moving to Roanoke, Maggie felt her tentative hold on control slipping, as vulnerability took its place.

"Cassidy wanted to wrestle during recess and I got in trouble."

The recess incident resulted in a tiny scratch on Matt's shoulder. In Matt's mind, though, it was the size of Iowa. Jared knew that one thing he and Matt shared was the struggle with forgiveness.

"Why didn't you just walk away?" Jared asked.

Like Jared should be doing: walking, no, *running,* away from Cassidy's mother.

"I tried, but she runs faster than me."

The tires on Jared's truck easily traveled over the new snow on Main Street. The first hint of a gray twilight was beginning to fall in Roanoke, and Jared was tired. The talk he'd had last night with his brother had given him reason to lose sleep. Yes, he'd been with Maggie Tate Friday night, Saturday night and all Sunday afternoon. No wonder Ryan thought they were dating. All Jared needed to do was get through the Christmas program and he could easily avoid Maggie.

"Hey," Caleb said, "I see a police car."

Jared slowed, fairly unconcerned. For the last few months, ever since seeing an old episode of *Adam-12,* Caleb had decided he wanted to be a policeman. On drives to town, he looked for the chief's police car. And, when possible, he went up to the chief of police and said, "I'm going to be a cop someday."

Alex Farraday always said, "Good, then Roanoke will have six cops instead of just five and I can spend more time at home with Susan."

Susan was Beth's sister. Jared was just glad Caleb hadn't been swayed by Joel into becoming a bull rider.

"It's in front of Cassidy's house," Matt noted, the scratch the size of Iowa momentarily forgotten.

Jared didn't hesitate. He quickly traveled the remaining block and parked across the street in front of Roanoke Rummage. Leaning across the seat, he rolled down the passenger-side window. Henry stood in the doorway, Cassidy right next to him, both looking out through the glass door like two kids denied access to candy.

"What happened?" Jared called. "Is Maggie all right?"

Henry opened his store's door a bit. "She got broken into while they were at the school. I heard a car pull away, and a

Once Upon a Christmas

minute later noticed her door was open. I called the police right away. I'm watching Cassidy but haven't seen or heard anything since Maggie and Farraday went inside."

"I think my presents got stolen," Cassidy complained.

Jared hurriedly rolled up the window, scooted his boys out of the backseat of the truck, and gave them to Henry. "I'll be over as soon as I know something."

Henry merely rolled his eyes good-naturedly and opened the door to his shop. For once, Ryan got with the program and moved. Matt even managed to look a little worried. Caleb's eyes lit up. Roanoke Rummage was full of junk and, as an added bonus, Cassidy was there, too.

The snow crunched underfoot as Jared made his way quickly toward Maggie's shop. It didn't escape him that just a few minutes ago he'd been congratulating himself for knowing enough to run away from her but now, here he was running toward her, as fast as he could. It also didn't escape him how worried he felt. After all, she was a friend, and he'd stop to help a stranger.

In his gut he knew he'd never felt this level of concern over a stranger.

When he stepped inside Hand Me Ups, the first thing he noticed was Farraday, a smile on his face, bent over, lifting fingerprints from the glass counter. "What's so funny?"

"I wish I had a surveillance camera on the thieves right now. Maggie says they took wrapped presents from under this tree and that all she'd done was wrap empty boxes for decoration. Picturing them opening empty box after empty box is something to smile about."

"Not everything they got was empty," Maggie said glumly.

"You all right?" Jared asked. He went to her and enveloped her in his arms, surprised when she let him. Gone was the Maggie Tate who was always in control, always seeing the glass half-full, and always ready with a smile or joke.

He held a woman who wanted to hit something, but since there were no punching bags available, she let him hold her.

He liked that.

"Of course I'm all right, we're all right." Her voice shook with anger. "I was at school while this happened. But they took some of my inventory, some personal jewelry and Cassidy's presents."

Farraday sobered right up. "You're right, it wasn't just empty boxes they took, and I'm sorry. You're the tenth victim, and I have no idea who'd be so brash as to park in front of your shop in broad daylight, and break in. But, your break-in is a bit different as they didn't get much and they left behind a clue." Farraday held up a baggy, as proud as if he were showing off his firstborn. "A screwdriver."

"You going for prints?" Jared asked.

"No, can't get prints from a screwdriver, not really, especially one as small as this, but it's an unusual and very old screwdriver. It gives me something to trace."

"They left it in my door," Maggie said, backing out of Jared's embrace.

"It got stuck in the cylinder of the mortise lock," Farraday said.

"That's a pretty old lock." Jared looked at Maggie's door. "You need something newer, stronger."

"It was plenty strong. After all, the screwdriver got stuck," Maggie debated.

Jared didn't laugh.

"He's right," Farraday agreed. "Plus, a Christmas tree right by a window is an open invitation."

Jared watched as Maggie flinched. Her lips went together, and he wondered what she was thinking. After a moment, she said, "Every business on this street has a tree in their front window. It's called good marketing. We rely on our neighbors keeping watch and our police department doing its job to keep us safe. By the way, if you don't find my daughter's presents, she's not getting any. Is that clear enough, chief?"

Aah, the cat had claws.

"Henry says his wife heard a car," Jared put in.

"I planned on talking to him after I leave here. You mind if I go upstairs and look again? See if anything else is missing?" Maggie asked.

At Farraday's nod, Maggie went upstairs and Jared headed for the door. "Okay if I touch it?"

"Go ahead. I'm about done."

Jared studied the lock. "It's destroyed."

"The lock probably was worth more than what they got away with," Farraday said soberly.

"Maggie said jewelry."

"Most of it she claims she made herself. It was spread out on the coffee table next to the tree. My guess is they saw it and made a sweep because it was convenient. The value comes from selling it for more than it cost to make. By her estimate, the only reason she's in the hole is because some items she had on consignment were taken and now she feels obligated to pay the vendors."

Together, Jared and Farraday righted the tree and secured it in the base. Soap ornaments fell at their feet. Once that was finished, Jared looked at the door. "Think Bob's Hardware will have a replacement?"

"He might, but you're going to be looking at more than two hundred dollars. Plus, for that kind of lock, you'll need a locksmith."

"I can do it."

"Looks easy, I know, but believe me, the mortise is not the easiest lock to mess with."

Jared headed to his truck. Thanks to what he was doing at school with the scenery, most of his tools were in his truck bed toolbox. No one was looking out the entryway of Roanoke Rummage. Either interest had died or Henry had his hands full supervising four children.

Jared got down the measurements and ascertained that it was a right-handed doorknob. Maggie came down the stairs. "No, everything is there. I'm going to get Cassidy and bring her home. She'll be worried."

"Grab my boys, too," Jared said. "If they can stick around a moment, I'll run to the hardware store and get you a lock."

Maggie stopped just short of her counter, took a breath, and said a soft "Thank you." Jared thought about going to her and wrapping his arms around her to tell her everything would be all right. If ever there was a woman who needed someone to hold her, it was Maggie, right now. If she'd been anybody else, he would have.

If she'd been anybody else, ulterior motives would not be questioned, especially by the man giving the hug.

But he didn't move.

And the moment vanished into regret before Jared had the wherewithal to realize a missed opportunity.

Plus, he wasn't sure who needed the hug more. Maggie or him. Maggie because she was scared. Jared because he was scared for her.

It had been a long time since he'd been scared for a woman.

Chapter Twelve

Maggie made homemade pizza for everyone. It was the only thing she had that would feed seven, since Henry had stayed. While she rolled out the dough, she tried to keep her eyes on Cassidy instead of the empty place under the tree. Someone had invaded her space, had taken things that didn't belong to them, and had made her feel like she was losing control.

Again.

Prayer would help. She knew it would, and if there was ever a day when she needed to talk to God, it was today. But when she tried to form the words, the thoughts, all she got was emptiness.

Having an apartment full of people was somewhat reassuring but it was also overwhelming. It had been just her and Cassidy for so long, even when Dan was alive because he was gone so often.

She wasn't quite sure how to respond to all this help.

Cassidy, of course, loved it and felt like she was a princess and everyone in the apartment was there to worship her. She and Matt did their homework at the kitchen table amid the smell of pizza sauce and garlic. Every once in a while, Cassidy leaned over to check what Matt was doing. Matt responded by shielding his work. After calling his wife, Tess, Henry sat with them. "She says she'll come over another time. Right now she's tired and just wants to go to bed."

Maggie wondered why she hadn't invited them over sooner. "I'll send a couple slices of pizza home with you."

Henry nodded as he admired Matt's handwriting and recommended that Cassidy start over.

"Help me," was Cassidy's suggestion.

And he did.

Ryan sat in the tiny living room watching television and watching Maggie.

"Want to help me spread the sauce?" Maggie asked.

"No."

"Put the pepperoni on?"

"No."

"Throw it up to the ceiling and see if it sticks?"

"Yes," shouted Cassidy, almost falling out of her chair. Caleb, on the floor surrounded by Cassidy's collection of toy horses nodded in agreement. Ever the boy, he had the ponies battling each other for control of a pretend base. Yes, if Cassidy were a princess, then Caleb was a prince.

"Don't be silly," Ryan said.

"Being silly is fun," Maggie said. "And on a day like today, it's better than crying."

"I'm the one who should be crying," Cassidy said. "It's my toys that got stolen. And, not just toys, but red boots probably. Do you know how important red boots are?"

"And how hard to find," Henry agreed.

All the boys looked bewildered. Even Caleb checked out his own boots as if to see if they'd turned red.

"I'm the one who should be crying." Jared walked into the room, a hammer in his hand and a scowl on his face. "That lock was a bear to replace."

"I can't thank you enough," Maggie said. "How much do I owe you?"

Jared took off his coat and gloves, folded them and put the hammer on top before coming into the kitchen and peering over her shoulder at the slightly round creations ready to go in the oven. "Two pizzas ought to cover it."

She could smell snow and something else, aftershave maybe, something definitely male.

Henry raised a hairy eyebrow but didn't say anything.

"No, really." Maggie brushed flour off her hands, stuck the pizzas in the oven and headed for her purse.

"I have the receipt in the truck," Jared said. "I'll bring it in when we're finished eating."

She left her purse where it was and got busy with drinks and napkins. She froze, two drinks in her hand and another on the counter, off to the side while Jared said a prayer. The boys and Henry bowed their heads automatically. Cassidy bowed, waited a moment, looked around at all the people bowing, bowed again, but was too interested in everyone else to understand she should be listening.

After the "Amen," Maggie started breathing again. They weren't the best pizzas, but they weren't the worst, either. They were edible and hot, the only criteria in Maggie's kitchen. The kids gathered in the living room around the coffee table. Caleb and Cassidy ate everything handed to them. Matt ate one piece and complained about the sauce. Ryan complained about the sauce and went hungry. Good thing Jared thanked God before the meal because afterward might have been a different plea.

The adults were in the kitchen.

"I make my own sauce," explained Maggie. "That way I can control Cassidy's intake of Red Dye #40."

"That help?" Jared asked.

"It does, and luckily, since I'm not much of a cook, it's somewhat easy to make. I can send some home with you."

Jared hesitated a moment. "I took Caleb to the doctor today and came home with a bunch of paperwork, some of it just ideas, same as you mentioned to me before. We're going to see an allergy specialist tomorrow. Then, I'll need to call the Calcaw Center. I'm willing to try just about anything."

Seeing that both Matt and Cassidy were doing more listening than homework, Maggie turned to Henry and changed the subject, "Are there always some thefts around Christmas?"

"Some," Henry said. "But nothing like this year. And I don't remember presents being the target. Usually it was something like money from somebody ringing a bell for donations. One year someone broke into the church and stole the contributions."

"I remember that," Jared said. "You think it's the same person doing it now?"

"No." Henry didn't hesitate. "Both those times, it was one hit and over. This is a serial thief and they're targeting homes with children. I'm thinking it's someone new to town or someone from one of the neighboring towns."

"Someone from a neighboring town wouldn't know my schedule," Maggie pointed out.

"Maybe the thief didn't know your schedule but read the sign on the door and took a chance."

"So, you don't think they'll be back?" Maggie set down her pizza, half eaten.

"Not to your store," Henry said. "They got what they wanted."

"All the break-ins have been when the homeowners were gone," Jared reassured.

"Which is why I think it's someone local." Henry finished his pizza and then stared out the window. He took one finger and touched the center of the pane. "You need to replace this. You're losing good heat."

"I know," Maggie admitted. "It's on my list."

Henry took his plate to the sink and headed for the living room and his winter coat. Maggie didn't want Cassidy to think she had to worry about whoever had broken in coming back.

"I think it's someone local, too," she confided to Jared. "And I agree with Henry. They target people who have kids."

"So, toys are the goal?"

Maggie nodded. "They took my jewelry because it was convenient. I even had it lying on a towel. All they had to do was roll the towel closed. They took inventory that would make good Christmas presents."

"I think you might be right. You've been hit, the Totwells were hit. My neighbors, the McClanahans, were broken into a good three weeks ago while they were at church. I can't remember everyone else, but if we look, I'm sure kids and presents are the common denominator. Which is good, somewhat, because then you don't need to worry about them coming back."

"Dad! Caleb won't stop sticking his tongue out!" Matt hollered.

"It's time for us to go." Jared gathered up paper plates and napkins. He had his boys do the same. "We have homework and bedtime right around the corner. Thanks for feeding us."

"We enjoyed your company." It was true, too true. She was enjoying Jared's company more and more each time.

She didn't deserve it.

It wasn't until after everyone had left, Cassidy was in bed and Maggie was finishing up dishes, that she realized Jared hadn't returned with the receipt.

Sitting at her computer, she did a Google search for the lock but gave up. She couldn't remember what type Farraday had said it was, only that it was old.

Almost afraid, she went to her accounting software. She'd already giving Farraday a handwritten account of all that was missing downstairs. The thieves had hit the tree, grabbed presents and what she had nestled in that area, namely scarves, quilts and blankets, and had made off with more than five hundred dollars in handcrafted booty.

They'd taken the three presents under the tree. The boots had cost Maggie ten, the book three and the previously viewed DVD just under five. Eighteen dollars in all. At a time when eighteen might as well be a hundred.

The jewelry was nothing. She dabbled at jewelry making and someday wanted to do more with it. After all, she had a shop to sell it in. Right now, though, alterations paid the bills, homemade jewelry was just another impulse buy and a task she had little time to hone. Everything in her jewelry box had been homemade.

Her good jewelry was hidden. She'd already checked to make sure the Koa jewelry box Dan had given her the day they had married was still in the back of the closet inside her good suitcase.

Careful not to wake Cassidy, Maggie tiptoed into the bedroom and went into the closet, shutting the door behind her before she pulled the string to the light. It took a moment to move some quilts from on top of the suitcase, but then she held its contents in her hand. Of all the things Dan had given her, Cassidy excluded, this was Maggie's most cherished. At a time when money was tight, he'd spent all he had on a two-drawer, one-of-a-kind handcrafted box simply because she'd said she liked it.

He hadn't purchased the cheapest, either. He'd gotten her the one she'd wanted.

Settling cross-legged on the floor, she settled the Hawaiian jewelry box on her lap and tugged on one of the ebony handles. Inside was a necklace her mother had left behind. Maggie had no idea if it was worth anything or not. She also had no idea why she had kept it. There were at least a dozen earrings hanging in the tray back from her high school days and not her style any longer. Bracelets were crammed into the second drawer, not Maggie's favorites. Others had been left untouched on her dresser.

In the ring slot was just one offering.

She removed the ring from its black velvet resting place and rolled it between her fingers. It was yellow gold and not even a carat. Dan had purchased it online a month before getting the courage to ask her to marry him.

He'd loved her.

Made promises and kept them.

Maggie's tears came slowly at first. Guilt was a hard fist that didn't give way to emotions easily. But, after working all day, helping at the school, the break-in and then a whole household of people who called her friend, the guilt became an open wound. She was crying for Dan, but thinking of Jared.

She didn't deserve to have feelings for a man like Jared, a man who had loved his wife so much that if he ever married again, he wanted it to be to someone exactly like her.

Not exactly like Maggie.

When Dan had left for Afghanistan for his last tour, she'd waved goodbye at the airport and breathed a sigh of relief.

Because life was easier without him.

She was glad he was going. She prayed to God he'd be gone a little longer. She wanted to work on structure with Cassidy so that when Dan came back, there'd be no strife in the home.

She'd asked God to let Dan stay gone a little longer this time.

God had answered her prayer.

Dan was gone forever.

For the next couple of days, Jared made a point to drive by Hand Me Ups on his way to school and on his way from picking them up. A couple times he could see Maggie inside working, but she never noticed him.

At church on Wednesday evening, he sat in the auditorium class and for the first time, really looked around. For some reason the room looked brighter, the people more animated and more colorful. Everywhere there was a sense of happiness and togetherness.

Everywhere there were happy couples. Some were new couples, like his little brother and Beth. Some couples had been around a lot longer, like Henry Throxmorton and his wife, Tess. Jared knew exactly how long Henry and Tess had been together because right before Thanksgiving the church had thrown them a fiftieth wedding anniversary party.

Fifty years with one person. That was longer than Jared had been alive.

When Bible study ended, the kids filed into the auditorium for a short devotional. Matt liked to sit with Beth. Caleb moved from seat to seat, first sitting by Jared, then moving to Patty Maynard, the nurse who'd given him a sucker the other day. After a moment, and in a move that would do the NFL justice, he managed to quietly flip over the pew and sit next to the Totwells. He ended up crawling under the pew and leaning against Billy, whispering in his grandpa's ear and drawing him a picture. Ryan sat next to Jared.

Wednesday nights were always hard.

After church, Jared and Billy helped the boys into their jackets. Patty even stooped down to assist Caleb as she was leaving.

"I like you," said Caleb. "You don't do shots."

"Not always," Patty agreed.

"Sometimes we have to have shots," Matt said, ever practical.

Both Ryan and Caleb frowned at him. Even Grandpa Billy looked at Matt with a touch of concern and said, "But we don't have to enjoy them."

Patty chuckled. "I thought the lesson was good tonight."

Ryan tugged on Jared's shirt. "Let's go. It's getting late. I'm tired."

Now he became the target of frowns.

"You're never tired," Matt accused.

Billy gathered all three in front of him and pushed toward the exit. Jared put on his hat and took one step to follow, then paused.

He'd noted the sense of togetherness in the church tonight, and, yes, lately he'd been feeling restless. He turned and looked at Patty. "Say, Patty, how you doing?"

She was the kind of woman he should be asking out. She'd grown up on a farm, knew the life. She was a great-looking woman.

She was slow in answering. "I'm fine. And you?"

"Good."

They stared at each other for a moment. Then, Patty nodded before walking away as if understanding the question he hadn't asked.

The thought had crossed his mind to ask her out. A thought so obvious his oldest boy and stepfather had picked up on it.

But, if she was indeed the kind of woman Jared was looking for, he would have noticed before now.

By the time Jared got back to the farm with the family, it was after nine. Ryan and Matt got themselves to bed. Caleb was a bit more of a challenge. The later it got, the worse he behaved.

"He's tired," Billy said.

"So are the other boys." Jared actually had to fill the tub for Caleb's bath otherwise Caleb made the water too hot to step in. If he wasn't watched, he'd overflow the water, too.

"Every child is different."

Jared nodded. Caleb headed for the bath, all smiles, completely happy to be naked, completely happy to have help from Jared, because Caleb didn't remember Mandy at all.

Was that why Caleb was harder? Was it because he'd never had the feminine touch? After the bath, Jared helped dry off Caleb and put on his pajamas. Then, instead of rushing him to sleep, Jared sat on the edge of the bed and read a story from the Children's Bible, plus a Golden Book.

Caleb interrupted with questions, not about the stories. It took twice the time to read the books. Finally, Jared headed down the stairs, turned on the evening news and settled in his favorite chair.

"You want to talk?" Billy hit the remote so the television muted.

"Hey, I was watching that!"

"Really?" Billy asked. "Because the news ended ten minutes ago and you're watching a late-night talk show."

Jared looked at the television in disbelief. His stepfather was correct. Right now a parody on Santa made fun of the season. Not something Jared wanted to watch.

"So, where were your thoughts?"

After turning off the television, Billy sat down on the couch and waited. As an elementary-school principal, followed by taking over the raising of two rowdy boys, and now three rowdy grandsons, Billy was the epitome of patience. When Jared didn't volunteer to talk, Billy found something to say. "I guess Joel's still with Beth."

"He took her home from church."

"I know. That was about three hours ago. Guess they have a lot to talk about."

"He's in love."

"Not a bad thing," Billy said. "It certainly calmed Joel down, made him a happier person."

"Joel was always a happy person."

"No, he wasn't." Billy leaned forward and absently straightened the coffee table. His hair was fully gray now. It had been brown when he'd married Jared's mother. He was tall, taller than both Jared and Joel. He had a military walk but hadn't served. Instead of leading soldiers on the field, he'd lead in the school yard and at church.

"You should talk with your brother, really talk, find out why he left."

Jared felt the first touch of guilt. Joel had opened up about why he'd left and it all had to do with not feeling like he had belonged. Jared couldn't begin to understand his little brother's feelings, couldn't imagine walking away from family, from the farm, from commitments. Yes, Joel was back now and all was forgiven, but there were consequences to every action. The worst one for Joel was no longer having any ownership of Solitaire Farm. He'd sold his portion to Jared, at a time when Jared could least afford the purchase. There'd been some lean years for Jared and Mandy, especially when Mandy got sick and they had the mortgage to pay.

It wouldn't have been quite so hard if Joel hadn't wanted his money right away. Or if Jared hadn't had to take out a mortgage at the exact time he lost the brother who was supposed to work alongside him.

"Think about Caleb," Billy said. "What if he does something to make Matt and Ryan mad and they turn on him."

"I didn't turn on Joel!"

"Yes, you did."

This conversation was taking a direction Jared wasn't prepared for. "What? I did not. I was always there for him."

"You were always there. That's different than being there for him." Billy leaned forward, glaring at Jared, as serious as he'd been in years.

Jared was willing to fight this out, but the exhaustion he saw on Billy's face stopped him.

"Do you feel all right?"

"It's just the cold, hanging on. I've finally stopped coughing but I'm tired, my bones hurt and I'm worried."

"You don't have to worry about me. Joel's the one we

worry about." Jared tried to make the words light, but they didn't sound light.

"Not anymore. Joel's a good guy and he's found his place. It's your turn."

Jared looked around the living room. How could Billy say Jared needed to find his place? His place had always been here. The portrait over the fireplace held Jared's family. Years ago, the portrait had been of Jared, Joel and his parents. His grandfather, grandmother and dad had been there at one time.

Where was that painting?

The curtains over the big window were fairly new. Mandy, with the help of her girlfriends, had made them. Back then, the house had been full of voices and giggles.

Well, it still was, but the voices and giggles were his kids—mostly Caleb.

"I made a big mistake," Billy said, "when I asked you if I could marry your mother."

Jared straightened. "You know, if I'd gone straight to bed, like I normally do, we wouldn't be having this conversation."

"Not tonight, but soon. I've been planning on it for some time now."

"A conversation telling me you did wrong marrying my mother?"

"No, not by marrying your mother. That was the smartest thing I ever did. The mistake was when I called you into my office and asked your permission. I called you in because you were the eldest son. I'd watched you. When your dad died, the three of you McCreedys banded together. Your mom was mom and dad both. You took over the farm. I was amazed. You were just a teenager. You also took over raising Joel."

"He pretty much raised himself."

"No, he had you for an example."

"I'm not getting the mistake you're alluding to. Why was asking my permission a mistake?"

"Because I should have asked both you boys for permission. By asking just you, I left Joel out."

"He didn't feel…" Jared's words tapered off.

"Tell me," Billy asked. "When you proposed to Mandy and started getting ready to move her into the house, did you ever talk to Joel?"

"He was just a kid, still in high school. I don't remember. I don't think so. Why would I?"

"I think you might want to look at your own boys," Billy said. "Because change is coming, I can see it, and you need to talk to them, prepare them, and make sure they all feel included. Especially Ryan."

"If you're talking about Maggie Tate—"

"Maggie?" Billy's face had a look of fake surprise. "Isn't it Patty Maynard you asked out tonight?"

"Well," Jared stammered, "no, but almost…."

"It's not Maggie I'm talking about, although I wouldn't mind a bit should that happen. She'd make a fine wife for you."

"She's not—"

"Mandy? I noticed that, too. Neither is Patty Maynard. You've made Mandy a little too perfect in your memory. If you wait for another Mandy, you'll die alone."

"That's harsh."

Billy chuckled. "I'm not too worried. I think you're working your way back to the land of the living, maybe even missing the soothing touch of a woman's hand, the sound of her laughter. The Bible says it in Proverbs 18. *He who finds a wife finds what is good and receives favor from the Lord.*"

Jared's throat tightened. The scripture was spot-on. It had been good with Mandy. His whole world had felt right. Billy was spot-on, too. Jared missed having a woman by his side.

He wanted what he had with Mandy: someone who loved the farm, loved working side by side and loved him.

The only way he could have that was to find someone like Mandy.

Chapter Thirteen

There were shoppers and then there were hoppers.

Shoppers came to a store, strolled through the aisles, touched a few items, lingered for a caress or two, and then did it all again before finally settling on something to either try on or buy outright.

That's if the shopper was alone.

If the shopper came with a friend or friends, it was the same scenario, only because conversation took place between every step, the game took twice as long.

And usually resulted in twice the sales.

Hoppers were a different story. A hopper came to a store and meandered aimlessly through the aisles. Meandered was, in this case, a more frantic kind of walk. Aimlessly was a word shop owners avoided. Hoppers touched every item but didn't caress. Individual hoppers didn't repeat the process, mostly because they didn't want their hopper status recognized. Then, they'd leave the store with a *you don't have what I'm looking for* comment. Not true. A hopper wasn't really looking for anything but a way to kill time.

If hoppers came in a group, they were great fun. In a group, you had a chance for a sale because they might gang up on some real shoppers and speed up the process of making a choice. Or, one hopper might actually get guilted into making a purchase.

Maggie'd had a Thursday full of guilt-free hoppers and a cash register that was more register than cash. There were two weeks and two days until Christmas. Chief Farraday had been by twice to check up on her. He'd not found the thief.

Worry shadowed Maggie. A constant, sore reminder of how much she bore.

Alone.

Not just about replacing Cassidy's presents but also about paying rent and utilities. Christmas was supposed to increase sales, so what was going wrong?

"I'll take this."

Nothing like selling one scarf to boost morale.

After her customer left, Maggie typed in the keywords *Red Cowboys Boots* into her computer. She already knew what she'd find. The cheapest pair, before shipping, was twenty-five dollars. The pair that most resembled the ones stolen were seventy-five.

If she purchased the twenty-five dollar pair, that was it, all there was for Christmas.

It was her only choice.

Not her only choice.

Maggie slowly tugged her cell phone from the side pocket of her purse. The number she needed was on speed dial. This was absolutely *not* what she wanted to do.

Usually all she battled for was control, but now she knew that alongside control was a battle for pride, and she was about to lose hers.

For Cassidy's sake.

She hit number two on the pad and listened as the connection made. Her fingers curled around the phone and her lips starting forming the words she needed to say. *Kelly, we had a break-in and we need help so that Cassidy will have a Christmas.*

In the back of her mind came the briefest beginning of a prayer. *Father, please help me make the right choice….* That's as far as she got. After all, really, Maggie had made the right choices. She'd worked hard and saved so that Cassidy would have a Christmas. She'd been frugal and diligent. She'd foregone things like going out to eat, and getting her nails done. Whatever was on free television was good enough for her. Some other lost soul had chosen the easy way— breaking into homes and taking what they hadn't worked for.

The words "This is Kelly Tate. I am unavailable. Please leave a message…" came on the recording at the exact moment Jared walked through the front door. Maggie wasn't sure which pleased her more—that she didn't have to talk to Kelly or that she did get to talk to Jared.

Only Jared wasn't walking through the front door. He was holding it open—letting the cold air in!—and examining the lock.

"It's working just fine?"

"Yes, and you forgot to give me the receipt so I can reimburse you."

Great, say the first thing that comes to mind when it would have been smart to hope Jared's forgetfulness lasted until after Christmas.

Something that looked a lot like understanding flickered in his eyes and Maggie felt a strange tightening in her chest. "What?"

"I didn't say anything." Jared honestly looked confused.

"Well, you had this look in your eyes."

He closed the door behind him and came into the shop, stopping in front of her, almost as if sizing her up. "I would say that I didn't mean to have the look, but since I have no idea what look you're talking about, I'd be lying."

Maggie didn't blush often. Growing up with just a father and his crew of friends could harden a girl. Then, with Dan, there'd been more of the same.

So why was she blushing now?

"I was in town," Jared explained, "and thought I'd stop by to see if the lock worked and if everything was okay."

"The lock works. Everything is okay. Farraday's been by twice already."

He looked at the door, and not in a way that made her think he was checking out the lock again. More in a way that made her think he wanted to escape. She didn't blame him.

"How much do I owe you?" she repeated.

"Call it a Christmas gift."

So, the look had been real. "No, you barely know me."

"I owe you for offering me advice about Caleb and for the pizza sauce."

"I haven't given you any real concrete advice, and I gave you pizza sauce that two of your boys won't eat."

"I can take a rain check on the advice, and they'll eat if they're hungry enough." Jared looked at his watch. "I'm on my way to pick up Caleb. We're driving into Des Moines. I'm running early so thought I'd stop by here. I just keep thinking this is something I've done by not paying enough attention to him. Or maybe it's because he's only had men around."

"You want to be sure," Maggie said gently.

"Lately, I'm not sure about anything."

Boy, Maggie knew that feeling, especially today, especially about this man. He had no clue the emotions he aroused. But he was here to talk about Caleb. That she could handle.

Her phone sounded. Usually, she checked the ID before answering, but not this time.

"I see you called," Kelly Tate said.

"Yes, I did."

"Have you changed your mind about coming for Christmas? It's not too late. Of course, plane fare will be higher now, but I'm willing to pay."

"Hold on just a moment." Maggie smiled at Jared. "I'm going to run upstairs and take this call. It's really important."

"I think I'll look around."

"My shop?"

"Sure," he said easily. "I have time, and I still have a few presents to buy."

"Well, if a customer comes in, do your best to sell something." Maggie could only hope as she hurried up the stairs. He'd have to buy the whole shop or sell the whole shop in order to save her from what she was about to do.

Out of breath, Maggie sat at the kitchen table and pushed Cassidy's breakfast plate out of the way. Her daughter was supposed to put her dirty dishes in the sink. "Kelly, someone broke into the shop the other night and—"

"Is everyone all right?"

Maggie had to give Kelly credit. She'd asked if *everyone* was all right, not just Cassidy.

"We're fine. But, they took the Christmas presents. The police think it's someone targeting families and specifically toys."

"I'm so relieved you're all right."

"I've been on the computer all day. Cassidy wants a pair of red boots. I had them under the tree."

Silence.

"I can't afford to replace them."

"Just one pair of red boots?" Kelly's tone said it all. "Such a small request and you can't afford to replace them?"

Maggie started to sprout statistics about starting a business, being a single mom, but Kelly didn't let her finish.

"If you'd opened your shop here in New York, I'd have helped every step of the way. You could have lived with me and I'd—"

"Kelly, I always appreciated the offer, but Manhattan is not for me. I've always dreamed of living in a small town."

"Dreams don't pay bills."

Downstairs, someone pushed open the front door and a bell chimed.

Sometimes they do, Maggie mouthed the words. Aloud, she said, "I just need a loan. Two hundred dollars. I'll pay you fifty a month for four months."

"The boots cost two hundred dollars?"

"Nooo." Maggie knew full well Kelly knew the money was for boots and more.

"I can buy Cassidy the boots and send them. What size is she now? A three?"

Maggie cleared her throat, gave Kelly the brand and web-site address for the pair Cassidy really wanted and affirmed, "Yes, she's a three."

"Okay, then, that's settled."

Maggie nodded. She had the boots, but she didn't have the money to pay her customers what was owed them. And there'd not be much else under the tree.

Right now it was pretty hard living a dream.

A different woman came down the stairs. Maggie Tate, a woman who consistently seemed in control, had gone up. That's what he always noticed about her. She managed to conquer whatever obstacle life threw at her whether it be missing lunch boxes or missing Christmas presents. But the woman who came down the stairs was a lost soul.

"Are you okay?"

It didn't take a rocket scientist to realize that whatever the phone call had been about, she wasn't going to tell him and it obviously hadn't been good. It really wasn't his business. But he couldn't remember the last time he'd seen a woman look this...this tightly wound.

The closest was Beth, telling him that she thought some-thing was wrong with Caleb's attention span.

No, not even close.

Lately, all Jared's strife was about his boys. Working Solitaire Farm had been easier since Joel's return. Two pairs of hands made twice the work and divided the time. Plus, Joel's ideas had brought in more money.

Whatever was bothering Maggie ran deep. Interfering was the last thing he should do but, at the moment, he'd do anything to put a smile back on her face. "I'm early picking up Caleb and have an hour to kill," he said. "I'm taking you to lunch."

She was shaking her head before he even finished speaking.

"I knew you'd say no. That's why I didn't ask. You need a break, and I'm hungry. When we come back, I'm finishing up my Christmas shopping. I found the perfect coat for Billy." To prove it, he pointed to the first coat on a rank of men's coats in the back of the store.

Her quest last month for a 1930s denim chore jacket for George Maynard had resulted in a few finds that didn't work for him. They were good coats, though, bargains, and Maggie simply hung them up and waited for the right buyer.

"Billy's a big man?"

Jared looked at the coat again. "Well, he's tall."

Walking over, Maggie took it off the rack and handed it to him. "I think it will fit you." Any other day, there'd have been a sparkle in her eye as she tried to sell him something as ridiculous as this old coat. But today, the very stillness, seriousness, of her actions made him careful in how he responded.

It was the first time he saw Maggie Tate as fragile.

The brown insulated parka he wore quickly left his shoulders. She helped him into the bluish striped chore jacket so big on him that the collar came up to his nose. The sleeves hung past his fingers. "If I zip it up, it could be a tent instead of a jacket."

Then, she giggled, and he knew he had her.

"Okay, it's not you. And, I doubt it's Grandpa Billy, either."

"Billy does need a work jacket, though," Jared said. "And you've got some that will work. You can show me one when we get back."

She had that look in her eyes, the I-gotta-get-out-of-here look that females sometimes get when the day has been too long, the kids too loud and the expectations too high.

Jared was glad he happened to be in the right place at the right time.

He wanted to rescue her.

"Who was at the door?" she asked.

"Henry wants you to run over when you have time."

Ten minutes later they were in the Red Barn Grille, the restaurant his family occasionally came to on Sundays after church. It was the nicest one in town, looked like a restaurant from the Wild West days and served home-style meals.

Jared stepped through the door expecting to feel instant guilt. After all, he'd brought Mandy here while they were dating, while they were engaged, as newlyweds and then with children. To his relief, it was like last night at church. The lights seemed a bit brighter, maybe due to the addition of Christmas bulbs and sparkling icicles. The people seemed just as animated, and he couldn't help but notice how many couples there were.

It was noon and the place was half-full.

It didn't escape his notice that he was with the prettiest woman in the room.

The hostess looked surprised. After they were seated, Jared saw that quite a few of the staff, both front and back, peeked out to see who he was with.

When his favorite waitress showed up, menus and water glasses in hand, and a way-too-happy smile on her face, he introduced Maggie as a friend, the mother of a student in

Matt's class and someone working with him on the school's Christmas program.

Hillary, who'd been serving him chicken fried steak since he was ten, simply nodded and said, "Sure, honey. She's all that." Turning to Maggie, she said, "I don't think I've seen you in here before. Are you new in town?"

"Fairly new. We arrived in June. I purchased the building across from Roanoke Rummage. Maybe you've seen it. Hand Me Ups."

Hillary nodded. "Been meaning to come visit. I like old clothes."

"Every time I've driven by here, I've thought about coming in. We like good food."

"We?"

"I have a seven-year-old daughter."

"Glad you waited for a special occasion." Hillary patted Jared on the shoulder. "Next time bring the little girl."

Jared saved Maggie from having to answer. "We need a few minutes." He set down his menu. He always got the same thing. Fried chicken. Billy couldn't make it so if the McCreedy men had it for dinner, it came from a box. Not the same as homemade.

Settling back, he enjoyed watching Maggie peruse the menu. She was still way too serious but no longer fragile-looking. He checked his watch. She wasn't in a hurry, either. "We've got maybe forty minutes before I need to pick up Caleb."

"Just enough time," she agreed and went back to the menu.

Okay. He looked out the window. It wasn't snowing, but what they'd had earlier in the week had turned to slush and mud. Alex Farraday, chief of police, drove by slowly.

Main Street didn't experience much of a rush hour on Thursday afternoons. Bob's Hardware Store had two or three people exiting its door. Jared only recognized one. Kyle Totwell. The other two people exiting the store were hidden behind a giant Christmas tree box.

Saps.

Roanoke Rummage was open, but Jared couldn't see anyone going in or coming out. The cold did that to people: inspired them to stay home. Christmas got them out, but it was still two weeks away. Plenty of time.

Jared flipped the menu to the back and skimmed the history of Roanoke again. He'd read it a few times before. He could read it again.

"I'm ready."

With the instincts of a seasoned waitress, Hillary knew right when to return and soon two salads appeared, plus a coffee and iced tea. Maggie picked up her fork and aimed it at the salad.

"You know," Jared said softly, "I usually say a prayer before eating. Would you join me? I promise to make it short."

"Go ahead," Maggie said softly. "Say your prayer." Jared kept his promise—short and simple. Yet, he noted that she didn't bow her head or close her eyes. She looked a little white knuckled.

Something about religion had turned off Maggie Tate, and since he wasn't sure what it was, he had to be careful.

Right after the *Amen* she started eating, slowly, delicately and deliberately.

"So, you want to tell me what upset you back there?"

She raised one eyebrow. "I wasn't upset."

"Yes, you were."

She huffed a bit, looking cute and vulnerable at the same time. She stared out the window.

Great, if he wanted conversation to happen, with this usually very free-with-her-words female, he'd have to instigate.

"I have a lot of respect for you," he finally said. "I can't imagine what it's like to be a single mom and have to do everything. The way you handle Cassidy is amazing."

"I don't handle her, I guide her, but thanks. You're a single father, with three sons. You know exactly what I'm going through."

"I know the frustration and the time spent. I know the joys and feeling of accomplishment. But I don't have to do everything. When Mandy passed away, Billy stepped up to the plate. I never had to worry. My boys have both Billy and me to guide them, as you say. Now, Joel and Beth are in the mix, too."

"You're lucky."

"It's more than luck. God's been with me every step of the way even when I wasn't looking to Him or asking Him for help. Where's your family? Beth said you might have relatives here, but she wasn't sure."

"Beth's a good friend, and she listens." Maggie returned to her salad. End of story. Jared wasn't sure if it was the family references or the God reference that made her go silent so he switched topics. "Caleb and I have a four-o'clock appointment in Des Moines. We're going to the Calcaw Center and meeting with a developmental pediatrician. Beth filled out three pages of forms. So did I."

"The first visit is easy. They'll do pretty much what your primary physician did. Caleb will get weighed, measured and observed. They'll ask you some questions, too."

"Like?"

"I don't remember everything from the first visit. Dan was with me and he wanted there to be a cause for Cassidy's behavior. Someone told him she was allergic to food. He liked that idea because then there was a fix. She had every test under the sun. No allergies. Meeting with the developmental pediatrician meant there were questions about Cassidy's bedtime, what she ate and how often, and if she had a temper. What we did to redirect her behaviors. Things like that."

Hillary came, took away their dirty dishes and filled their drinks.

Jared nodded. "Caleb's my difficult child when it comes to bedtime. He's got thirty different things he wants to do before getting under the covers and then he wants to talk when it's story time."

"You're lucky to get an appointment this fast. It took me three months to schedule the first appointment."

"There was a cancellation and I was on the call list. Good thing it's winter. I can get away a lot easier."

"I've always wondered what farmers did in the winter."

"From May to November, we often work fifty to sixty hours, seven days a week. So, the first thing we do is recoup from all the hard work. Then, I play catch-up on things like home and equipment maintenance. Of course, with Joel home, there's not so much to do. He fixes things the minute they break and he's fast. Me, I let them go until I have time and then it takes me forever to get them working again."

"Joel's a good guy."

"You're the second person to say that this week."

"Who was the first?"

"My stepfather. I wasted a lot of years being mad at Joel."

"Why?"

"After our father died, I pretty much took over the farm. The older Joel got, the more help I expected from him and the less he seemed to do."

"I'm an only child. I always wanted a brother or sister to do things with, to argue with."

Their main course arrived. Jared took a drumstick from his plate. Maggie took one from hers.

There'd been a time when Jared never figured to have Joel back in his life. Now, every time Jared turned around, Joel was there, making some outrageous demand. Last year it had been, *let me move home and take care of me while I heal.*

Then, it was, *I'm staying, bro, and marrying Beth Armstrong. You can be my best man. Oh, and you get to wear spats. By the way, can I bring her here as my wife to live on Solitaire Farm? It's a big house.*

And recently, Joel's crowning achievement—*take Maggie Tate to buy a Christmas tree.*

Joel didn't always get what he wanted. Jared wasn't wearing spats.

And, lunch today was purely Jared's doing. Joel couldn't take credit at all.

Maggie finished her first piece, took a sip of her coffee and started a second. "So, are you going to sell Joel back a piece of property or what?"

Jared almost choked. Hillary had to stop and pat him on the back. "About time someone got him excited," she commented.

Jared gave both of them a dirty look. Lots of people asked what he intended to do. None were so explicit. "No."

"The wedding's in three weeks and two days," Maggie reminded. "You going to have them move in with you when they return from their honeymoon?"

"Joel will have to figure something out."

"Yes, there are apartments available in town," Maggie said brightly.

Jared scowled and changed the subject for the third time. "So, what had you so upset earlier?"

Maybe it was that her stomach was full, maybe it was the adrenaline three cups of coffee provided, or maybe Maggie just needed someone to talk to. Jared didn't know, but Maggie finally slumped back and said, "I guess it doesn't matter—brothers, sisters, only children—we all have times when family drives us crazy."

Jared nodded.

"My mother-in-law," Maggie continued. "I called her today. She's the only family I have. We lived with Kelly in New York until six months ago. She didn't want us to move here, alone, so far away...."

"And?" Jared encouraged.

"I asked her if I could borrow money. I want to replace the cowboy boots that were stolen and have a bit more for Christmas."

"And?"

"She's sending boots but no money. She thinks if she doesn't send me money, eventually I'll have to move back in with her. That way she can be near her granddaughter. The only weapon she has is money."

"I'm sorry. I've been there. I purchased Joel's share of Solitaire Farm right after Ryan was born, and believe me, I wasn't making enough to pay the mortgage. Then," Jared's voice choked, "when Mandy got sick, if it weren't for Billy, we'd have lost everything."

"Well, I don't have a Billy, and my mother-in-law might win."

"No, you're a strong person and this is just a setback. We all have them. Some of us more than others. Don't give up hope. I know Alex Farraday. He's taking this personally. If anyone can find what's been stolen, it's him."

"Never give up hope," Hillary said bringing over the bill and gathering the dirty plates.

"I've been telling myself exactly that." Her voice sounded funny, sultry, and all Jared wanted to do was reach over, take her hands in his, and since he couldn't fix her problems, he wanted to pray. Automatically, he bowed his head.

"What are you doing?"

Her voice sounded funny again, but not strangled, more concerned.

He finished before answering, "I'm praying."

"For me?"

"For you."

"Oh, don't. Please. I can take care of myself."

He reached across the table and took her hand. Her fingers were warm to his touch. She'd painted the nails a bright pink.

She had rings on her pinkies and one on her thumb. The area on her wedding-ring finger was no longer pale or indented.

He looked at his wedding-ring finger.

There'd never been an indentation or a pale circle. He'd been too afraid of losing it or of getting it caught on a piece of machinery to wear it. And, he was quite fond of his finger, more so than any wedding ring.

Hillary stopped at the table, picked up the bill and money and looked at him. "Need change?"

"It's all yours," he said.

She looked at Maggie. "Jared left me a pretty good tip. Now I'll give you one. Best place to learn about hope is church. Look up Romans 12:12."

Maggie's eyes followed Hillary's but her expression didn't change even as she pulled her fingers from his. "What does Romans 12:12 say?"

"Rejoice in hope, be patient in tribulation, be constant in prayer."

"Sometimes I have a handle on the first two," Maggie said.

"The last one is the most necessary."

She gave the briefest shake of her head and said, "I need to get back to work."

He looked at the clock on the restaurant's wall. It was past time to pick up Caleb.

"You've made me late again," he accused, but he didn't care.

This time, it was worth it.

Chapter Fourteen

Maggie turned the Open sign so the public could see it. Lunch with Jared had been, well, interesting. She'd seen a side to him that surprised her. He'd been more open. He'd been not only sympathetic but empathetic, not something the men in her world excelled at, and he'd—typical male— offered concrete advice during their drive back to her shop.

Namely that she let him introduce her to the elders of the Main Street Church. They had a benevolent fund and he'd vouch for her.

Go to the church for money. Not a chance. She was still feeling a bit sensitive over the silent prayer he'd offered. She hoped it didn't backfire.

Maggie jogged up the stairs, grabbed a bottled water and came back down. There were still two hours before Cassidy got out of school. Hopefully there'd be a rush of customers. If not, she'd get some sewing done. Her goal: five elf hats and Mrs. Youst's sweaters. The elf hats were mindless. The sweaters, well, Cassidy's teacher loved sweaters but didn't like the size tag in the collar. Consequently, she pulled off the tags, managing to leave minute tears along the seam— tears that soon spread into unraveling big enough to put a

fist through. Good thing for Maggie because they were quick
and easy fixes. Too bad they didn't pay more.

Then, too, Maggie needed to do some of the final touches
on Beth's wedding attire. Their final fitting was scheduled
for Saturday at 9:00 a.m., an hour before the store opened.

Jared hadn't made it to the first fitting. It had been during
the final harvest. Beth had measured him at the farm and
then reported to Maggie.

The next hour passed with three customers and two very
profitable phone calls. One from a bride needing alterations
starting in January. Good, something to look forward to and
weddings paid well. The other from a doctor wanting to know
if she did custom shirts. She'd said yes but not until after the
New Year. She could learn that quickly if she had to.

Just before three, she closed the shop and headed for the
school. She needed to confirm she'd fulfilled her obliga-
tions, make sure Cassidy was doing what she was supposed
to, and if she were lucky, there'd be some over-extended
mom willing to pay to have a costume made. Maggie's fingers itched to get busy.

A few hours ago, they'd not itched. They'd been caressed.
By Jared McCreedy. What was he thinking? Maybe he felt
sorry for her. She hated that. Immediately, Maggie felt con-
trite. He'd been concerned, that's all. She'd been visibly upset
after talking with Kelly.

Yes, that had to be it. She wondered how he was making
out. About now, he'd be sitting on a sofa across from the developmental pediatrician and hearing what others—Beth and
now the pediatrician—had written about his child.

It was never easy. Maggie didn't even want to think about
her and Cassidy's next appointment at Calcaw. It wasn't for
another three months.

Roanoke Elementary was bustling. Kids knew it was just
a matter of days until no school and new toys. Cassidy wasn't
the only kid flying.

Later, back at Hand Me Ups, Maggie settled Cassidy at the kitchen table with her homework before heading back down to work in the shop a little longer. She'd love a last-minute sale or two. She'd just settled behind the counter and picked up one of Mrs. Youst's sweaters when the door opened.

Henry, for the first time, had a smile that crossed his face. She saw the man he must have once been, young and vital. In his hands, he carried a stained and wrinkled brown grocery sack. "Cassidy around?" he said.

"I can get her."

"No." Furtively, he came to lean against the counter, checked the stairs, and then set down the bag.

Maggie felt the first stirring of surprise. "Did you bring me something?"

"Even better," Henry said.

Opening the bag, he tilted in toward her. She stood so she could peer in.

Red boots.

In even better condition than the ones that had been stolen.

"How? When?" Maggie felt like dancing, she felt like flying around the counter and giving Henry Throxmorton a hug. Instead, she hugged the bag containing the boots.

"I know every antiques and thrift shop in a five-city area. I emailed the owners, told them what I was looking for and the size. I got two responses this morning. This is the pair that worked."

"How did you get them so fast?"

"Just so happened one of the owners was coming into town to visit a friend. He dropped them off."

"How much do I owe you?" Maggie's voice didn't waver at the words, although she acknowledged she'd asked that question more than once today. Come to think of it, the first time, she'd not received an answer.

Henry looked a bit sheepish. That's when Maggie noticed a second brown bag, just as stained and wrinkled as the first, tucked under his arm. "There's five pairs of men's trousers in here. One of them has a pin indicating where they need to be hemmed. He wants them all the same. I said if you couldn't do it, I'd call to let him know."

Her fingers had been itching earlier. Looked like she had something to scratch.

"Henry, I can't thank you enough." She danced around the counter and gave him the hug he deserved.

"Well," Henry said humbly, "it just took a few minutes on the computer and a couple of prayers."

Maggie thought about Jared's prayer.

Too bad he hadn't prayed before she had called her mother-in-law.

"I hear you found a pair of boots."

It had been almost seventeen years since Jared McCreedy had called a female on the pretense of small talk.

"I didn't. Henry did. They're wrapped and under the tree already." Maggie's voice lilted more like her old self but possibly a little guarded.

"I like Henry." Jared winced. He sounded a bit like his youngest son, not the image he was going for. This morning he'd decided it was time. He'd driven by her shop, made sure all the windows looked intact, fretted a bit about the snow needing shoveling from her walk and realized that she was taking too much of his thinking time.

It was almost noon now, and he'd admitted to himself that he couldn't stop thinking about her. Maybe he'd survive if it were summer. Then, he'd be forced to shake the feeling that he needed to stop at Hand Me Ups just because he drove by. If it were summer, not only would he be bone tired—and happy—as he tilled, fertilized, planted and sprayed, but he'd not be driving through downtown Roanoke when the sun was shining.

"How did yesterday go?" Maggie asked.

Jared waited his turn at a four-way stop. One other car was in the intersection. Yesterday, he'd waited his turn amid a slew of parents. "I wasn't prepared for the waiting room. Everything else was pretty much as you predicted."

The guarded tone left her voice. "What do you mean about the waiting room?"

"Look," Jared said. "I just dropped off some things at school, and I'm a minute away. Can I take you to lunch today? I do need to talk."

"I can't afford to close my shop again. Sometimes I get people on their lunch break who stop in to take a quick look and actually buy."

"I'll bring lunch to you."

"You don't have to."

"You're right. I don't have to. I want to."

She was quiet for a moment, and he imagined her face. She was a smart woman, had already been married, had a child. He was no longer a concerned dad wanting advice. He was a concerned dad wanting advice and realizing that the most beautiful woman in Roanoke had the most to say.

Had the most to give.

"All right," she said, "but if a customer comes in, they're my priority."

"I know how to share." He hung up the phone, headed for the Red Barn Grille and soon had two to-go orders of meat loaf and mashed potatoes. Not the most romantic of offerings, but good enough for a man who'd taken an hour to actually get up the courage to make the phone call.

It sure felt like asking for a date.

She had customers when he entered the shop, a mother and daughter it looked like. Used to be, Jared knew everyone in Roanoke. He nodded at them and got out of the way by setting the food at the end of the counter and shrugging off his coat, then pulled out the stool Maggie usually sat on from behind the cash register.

"I like that coat," the mother said looking at Jared's parka instead of the merchandise.

Maggie looked at him, a slow smile spreading across her face. "He's attached to it himself. Unfortunately, it's not vintage so I don't have any in stock. But, I had him trying on this one yesterday."

Both customers made a face at the blue striped 1930s denim chore jacket big enough to fit Santa Claus that Maggie pointed to.

"I want a coat for my husband. He keeps complaining he's cold." The woman spoke to Jared instead of Maggie. "We just bought the Calver farm. We want to try organic gardening."

"That's a good place," Jared said. "I've been there a few times back when Jack worked it. Right size if you don't add too many animals."

"We'll only do chickens," she said.

Jared stood and walked over to the women. "I was in here yesterday looking at coats. I'm going to buy my stepfather one. Here's the one I was thinking about."

He took a heavy jacket with John Deere stitched above the sleeve.

"Where do you work?" the mother asked. The daughter, realizing her mother was diverted, quickly sat on Maggie's stool and looked bored.

"I own Solitaire Farm." He stuck out his hand. "I'm Jared McCreedy."

"Oh! We've been there. Right, Celeste? We did the corn maze in October. We drove by a couple nights ago, thinking you'd have a Christmas maze going, but no. Why not?"

"My brother does Solitaire's Market. He's getting married in…"

"Twenty-three days," Maggie filled in.

"She's altering the wedding dress," Jared explained.

There was a bit more back and forth before the women

left the store with a good used coat, a bunch of soap and a crocheted shawl in their bags.

"I'm sad now," Maggie said, "that I didn't get Cassidy over to your place to do the maze. She asked. I saw it as just one more thing to do on a busy schedule."

"When Joel first put it together, it seemed like a waste of time to me, too. But, it's making money."

"We'll have to try harder to get there next time." Maggie opened one of the take-out orders and nodded. "I'm running upstairs for drinks and extra napkins. I'll be right back."

While she was upstairs, Jared moved her stool and found a second so they could both sit at the counter. He'd just started to sit down when the front door opened again. Clearly this was not going to be a peaceful meal.

"Hey, Jared," Henry greeted. "Saw your truck. You here to see the boots I found?"

"More or less."

Henry looked at the two meals on the counter. "You look pretty comfortable. Something I should know?"

"The meat loaf is on special today over at the restaurant."

"I don't need to go over there. My wife makes the best meat loaf known to man. You going to Mandy's folks for Christmas?"

Christmas. The holiday where families get together. Last Christmas they'd gone for the day. Billy came, too. Joel had already been courting Beth.

"I think they invited us."

"You think?" Henry smiled and shook his head. "You better find out for sure."

Maggie came down the steps, deposited what was in her arms on the counter and headed right for Henry. He got the kind of hug Jared had wanted when he'd walked in.

"Wife sent me over to see what you're doing for Christmas. It's just her and me, but we'd be proud if you and Cassidy came over."

"Henry, that's so sweet. Beth Armstrong already invited me to her sister's house."

"If you go to the Farradays'," Jared quipped, "at least your presents should be safe."

Neither Maggie nor Henry laughed.

"Did you hear about the preacher?" Henry asked, looking grave.

"No," Jared and Maggie answered together.

"Yesterday morning someone got in his house and took the present he'd wrapped for his grandson. They nabbed some cash, too, about fifty dollars."

"How many break-ins does that make?" Jared asked.

"We're up to eleven. And there's still just over two weeks until Christmas."

Henry left but not until accepting half of Maggie's meat loaf. She sat on her stool, one leg hooked over the other. How she managed to look comfortable was beyond Jared.

"Tell me about Calcaw," she said. "Especially what bothered you about the waiting room."

"First, I didn't like sitting there amid all those people I didn't know."

The waiting room had been about the size of Jared's living room and kitchen combined. He'd been given yet another form to fill out. Caleb was one of the youngest ones, but not by much. There'd been a sense of frantic motion in the room, but not from the kids. They were content to play their handheld video games or flit across the room from parent to aquarium to an activity corner and then do it all again.

"The seats were so close together." Jared had scrunched in a corner chair and again wrote down Caleb's age, address, school information.

After he'd turned in the chart, he listened to the parents around him. "These parents," Jared told Maggie, "were either seasoned professionals at doctor appointments or they were in shock."

"Which were you?"

"I didn't feel like either one. I felt like an imposter, like I didn't belong there."

"So what did you do?"

"Caleb was over by the aquarium, and I did the only thing I knew. I prayed."

"That this would all be a mistake." Maggie nodded.

"I won't deny that crossed my mind, big time. But mostly I prayed that every step I took would be the best step for helping him. I want him to do well in school, have friends, grow up to be successful."

"Then, why didn't you pray that what everyone's telling you is wrong? I know that's what I did." She finished her meat loaf, cleaned the counter around her and headed over to the trash can. She stood and looked at him, so serious.

"Between the books you recommended and Billy's advice, I just felt that I needed to offer up a different prayer."

"What did Billy say?"

"Billy said that most of us don't know what we ought to pray for, but that the spirit intercedes for us with groans that words cannot express."

Maggie blinked. "What exactly does that mean?"

"It's from Romans and means that God knows what is in our heart."

"God knows what's in our hearts," Maggie repeated. The thought didn't seem to make her happy.

"I've been reading those books you recommended," Jared said. "There's a chapter in one about kids who the parents thought had Attention Deficit but it turned out they didn't."

Maggie pressed her lips together. "You're on the chapter about autism."

"I'm praying that God watches me every step. He already knows my needs."

"But—" Maggie finally dropped everything in the trash

and then wiped her hands against each other "—if you make a specific prayer request, God answers. Right?"

"Yes," Jared acknowledged, "but the answer isn't always what we think it should be."

"Got that right," Maggie muttered, finally headed back to her stool and close enough that he could see the dark brown flecks in her green eyes.

"What?"

"The book is more help, right now, than God."

Jared shook his head. "Without God, the book wouldn't even be in my hands."

"What do you mean?"

His voice broke. "If I were to have a specific prayer, for while I was sitting back there in Calcaw's waiting room, I'd have been praying for Mandy to be right beside me. She always made everything so much easier. But, that's not a prayer God would answer. You want the honest truth? I didn't know what to pray for. One, I wanted out of there. Not going to pray for that. I need to thank God for places like Calcaw where there are specialists who know more than I do. Two, I wished you were with me. That's a prayer that scares me. See, I've not noticed a woman since Mandy died. And, lately I'm noticing you a lot. Now do you see why I pretty much just prayed that God would watch my steps? He knows my heart. He knows all about the first two petitions."

"He knows your heart," she said softly. "Well, He knows mine, too. And my heart is not worthy of yours." She stood, picking up the empty container in front of him and throwing it in the trash.

"My prayers…" Her voice went to a whisper as she headed for the front door and opened it, unmindful of the cold and letting him know it was time to go. Louder, she said, "My prayers were answered. I don't want to pray anymore, ever again, and that pretty much tells you that I don't belong anywhere near your heart or prayers."

Chapter Fifteen

Friday night Beth made dinner for the McCreedy men. She brought over Christmas presents, too, arranging them under the tree next to the ones Billy had already placed there. The fake ones she'd wrapped for her wedding were all sparkling, solid shades of red, gold and silver. The ones for the children all had Santa wrapping paper.

Both Caleb and Matt still believed. Ryan wasn't picking a side. Jared figured Ryan feared that discrediting Santa might result in fewer presents.

The biggest gift was for Joel. "I still believe," he said. But, he wasn't looking at the tree or the present, he was looking at Beth.

"I want the decorations still in place," Beth reminded. "Since my sisters are wearing burgundy, the bulbs on the tree and all the Christmas decorations will match." She looked at Jared. "Will the tree last that long?"

"I'll go get a fresh one from Paul if it doesn't." It amazed Jared that Beth didn't want a big wedding. He figured it had something to do with her mother still being in prison.

"Did you hear about the preacher?" Jared asked as the family gathered at the table. The extra leaf stayed in now that Beth was a frequent guest.

Beth nodded, but no one else did. Jared caught them up on the break-in at Michael Russell's house. Beth knew a bit more, thanks to her sister being married to Chief Farraday. She knew the gifts had been for a four-year-old boy. "Mike had just gotten a train set in the mail."

"Someone must have seen the postman deliver it," Billy said. "Mike never put his tree in the window."

"We need to move our tree," Ryan said. "So it can't be seen from the road."

"We're already too far from the road for it to be seen," Jared reassured.

"Can he order another train?" Matt wanted to know. "And, will it get here in time?"

"Santa will bring it," Caleb predicted.

"How'd you hear about all this?" Billy said.

"I was at Hand Me Ups having lunch with Maggie. Henry stopped by. He always seems to know just about everything that goes on in town."

"You ate with Miss Maggie?" Caleb asked. "Again? Did you have spaghetti?"

Matt rolled his eyes.

Ryan just looked at his food.

"Everything all right with her?" Beth asked. "She seemed a little down when I stopped by after school."

Jared gave a brief shake of his head. He'd talk to Beth later, not when the boys were around.

"She going to be done with the dress in time?" Joel asked

"I think so."

"You might want to find out. I'm leaving next week for Arkansas and the Elm Springs Rodeo. I'd like everything to be firmed up before I go."

"What's not firmed up, I'll take care of," Beth promised "Just remember that our fitting," she said, then looked around the room, "everyone's fitting is tomorrow morning at nine You do remember!"

Jared figured Billy was the only honest nodder.

"When's the next rodeo after Elm Springs?" Billy asked.

"New Year's Eve," Joel answered. "My wife and I will be attending together. Mr. and Mrs. Joel McCreedy."

Jared could only shake his head. Vagabond. That's what his brother was. And judging by the look in Joel's eyes, he was happier that he was taking his wife than getting to ride. Just wait until they had kids. He'd not be flitting here and there.

Of course, that's when he'd really be looking at Jared and talking about buying back, if not his share, then a few acres—enough to build a house and keep stock.

"Dad, Dad, I have a good idea. Can I give the preacher my train set from last Christmas?" Caleb asked.

Every adult paused, their eyes meeting across the table. Finally, Jared patted Caleb on the shoulder. The train set in question had been rode hard, put up wet and very loved. No way did Jared want to squash his son's giving nature. "We'll find out if that's needed when we go to church on Sunday."

The kids headed for the living room and the adults got busy. Joel went out to the barn to do animal duty. Billy settled down next to Caleb to work on letters. Ryan and Matt did their own homework.

Beth started gathering up the supper dishes. She didn't act surprised when Jared stood to work alongside her. "Why did Maggie stop going to church?"

"I don't know," Beth admitted. "It had something to do with the death of her husband. She's never really shared."

"He died in Afghanistan. Surely, she doesn't blame herself."

"I know how he died. I know she lived with his mother about six months and that she wasn't happy. I know she moved here because she always wondered if she might have family here. She found her mother's birth certificate. Her mother was born here. That's about all she's been willing to share."

"What was her mother's name?"

"Natalie Johnson. And her mother before that was Mary Johnson."

"There's two families at church named Johnson."

Beth nodded. "She spoke with them and with a few other families around town. We have plenty of Johnsons in Roanoke, just not the ones Maggie needs."

"How'd you meet Maggie?"

"That's your little brother's fault. She had hired Joel and I went along a few times. I was her first customer. Next thing I knew I'd made a friend. She knows more about clothes than anyone else. Plus, I love painting the murals on her walls."

"You're doing that in exchange for alterations."

"Yes," Beth said slowly, "but I pay her, too."

"Because she needs the money?" Jared guessed.

"She needs the money."

"I suggested yesterday that she go to our church and ask for help."

Maggie stopped wiping down the table and just stared at him. "I bet that went over well."

"Luckily, I suggested it while we were driving. She didn't answer, just stared out the window."

"That's typical Maggie. If she's uncomfortable with the subject, she gets quiet. It's how you know you struck a nerve. Anything else, she'll tell you what she thinks times two."

"So she never shares anything too deep?"

"I've heard about a few of the places that she's lived. And I know that Maggie was really hurt when her mom walked out on them."

"What kind of mom does that?"

Beth shook her head. "Maggie's one of the best moms I know. It's hard to believe she didn't have a good example."

Jared set the last of the dishes in the sink. "I pretty much told her that I was interested in her. And not because she's given me advice about Caleb and not because she has a child in my son's grade."

"Oh, Jared. I think that's wonderful. What did she say?"

"She said she didn't deserve my heart or my prayers. Then, she showed me the door."

"I told you she was afraid of God."

"Hmm," Jared said. "I think she's even more afraid of prayers."

"So, what are you going to do?"

"I'll fight fire with fire. I'll pray."

Saturday morning had Jared heading for his truck to make the group fitting appointment. He drove with Billy sitting next to him. Matt and Caleb were in the back. Ryan chose to ride with Joel in his truck.

"Three weeks until the wedding," Billy said. "Beth talk you into wearing those spats yet?"

"No. And there's two weeks until Christmas. Got all your baking done?"

Billy liked to cook but he hated to bake. Said it took up too much time. He was counting down to the wedding because when Beth moved in, she would take over making the sweets.

Once they got to Hand Me Ups, Maggie met Billy for the first time and let him flirt with her for all of a minute.

"So you're the one has my oldest boy coming to town often?"

She looked a bit stricken, at least to Jared's way of thinking, but she handled it well. "The way to a man's heart is through cooking, and he likes my pizza sauce."

Behind them both Matt and Ryan aimed their pointer fingers toward their mouths in a gagging motion.

Billy missed it. Jared and Beth did not. He licked his lips; she shrugged.

Then, Maggie became all businesslike. Not Cassidy. She

served as greeter, information gatherer and general gopher. The men went into the dressing rooms downstairs. Beth and her sisters went upstairs to Maggie's apartment.

Maggie remained downstairs to start with the men's suits.

To Jared's chagrin, his jacket, vest and pants fit perfectly. Once he had them on, Maggie barely had to run a hand across his chest and over to his side to see if the arms moved loosely enough.

He grinned; she blushed.

Then, she tucked a hanky in his pocket and scowled at his shoes.

"Not wearing spats," he said.

Joel's clothes were a little tight. "Nerves," he said jokingly. "I keep eating."

"It's because Beth is a good cook," Billy said.

Heading back into the changing room, Joel hesitated while Maggie went upstairs. "Ryan had a few things to say on the drive over."

"About Maggie?" Jared guessed.

"He doesn't like her. I told him I was surprised. We talked a bit more, and it's not so much he doesn't like her. He's afraid she'll be around more."

Caleb came from upstairs with Cassidy by his side. You'd think he was her personal doll. He'd been the lone male allowed in their ranks. His tiny tux fit perfectly.

"Mandy would have loved this," Jared said to Billy.

"Since she's not here, it's a good thing you know enough to enjoy it." Billy's phone rang. Flipping it open, Billy said a curt, "Hello."

That was followed with, "You're kidding….No, I'll bring the boys….Who's in charge of the meeting?…I'm with Maggie Tate now….Susan Farraday's here, too….I'll fill her in….I'm glad something's finally being done."

By the time Billy finished, all the bridesmaids were on the stairs, waiting. Only Beth couldn't come because she was in her wedding dress and Joel didn't get to see her in it yet. She hollered impatiently, "What's going on? It's cold up here. Who's on the phone?"

"What are you going to fill me in about?" Maggie carefully held the back of Susan's dress together. At eight months pregnant, Susan Farraday's prayer truly was that she'd lose weight by the time of her little sister's wedding: roughly eight pounds and six ounces.

Just in case she didn't, Maggie was dying a corset the exact same shade as the dress and adding part of it to each side of the zipper. She was also designing a wrap that would go perfectly.

"That was Mike Russell." To Maggie he added, "The minister at Main Street Church. There's a meeting tonight. The community is coming together to figure out what's been going on with the break-ins."

"Somebody else got hit?" Jared guessed.

"Your favorite waitress, Hillary. She got home from her shift last night and they'd taken everything under her tree. And she doesn't have the money to replace what was stolen by Christmastime. I think for the minister, Hillary was the final straw."

Jared heard Maggie's intake of breath and stepped closer to her. He put a hand on her shoulder. She didn't brush him off but she didn't give him any acknowledgment, either.

"Where's the meeting and what time?" she asked.

"Seven, and it's at the Main Street Church building."

"Why are they having it there instead of the school? Aren't most town meetings at the school?"

"This is last-minute. It's cheaper to heat the church, and the church offered," Billy said. "We were already having a prayer meeting."

"What can I do to help?" she asked next.

"What can we do to help?" came the sound of Beth and her sisters, all together.

"Call your husband and find out," Billy told Susan.

Susan took out the cell phone she'd tucked into the sleeve of her dress and made the call. When she hung up she said, "We need to spread the news."

"You need to do anything else on this dress?" Linda asked.

Jared had always liked Beth's oldest sister, Linda. She'd been in his class, and to his mind, she'd been the one to make sure little Beth was taken care of back when their mother had been way too strict.

Maggie shook her head.

"Then I need to get out of it and get busy. I'll make sure everyone who comes into my shop today for a hair appointment hears about the meeting tonight."

"Good," Susan said. "I'll head over to the police station and see if they've already made up flyers to hand out. I'll bring them over."

"No," both Beth and her older sister Linda said. "We can hand them out."

"I'm pregnant, not helpless."

"It's snowing and slippery," Billy toned. "You were always my best statistics student. Do the logic."

"Who invited him?" Susan grumped and turned to flounce up the last two stairs. Jared noticed that being eight months pregnant didn't hinder her from abrupt movement.

The fitting was now over.

"Why would Hillary be the last straw?" Maggie asked Jared quietly. "I mean, I'm glad there's being more action taken, but it seems a little strange. After all, the minister's a victim, too."

"Hillary's a success story. She had a rough beginning. Her folks, well, let's just say they didn't deserve to be parents. Hillary made a couple mistakes but somewhere along the line, she found God. I think she's like the widow in the Bible who gave God a single mite but it was everything she had."

Maggie nodded, understanding.

"Also, and this isn't so well-known, Hillary used the benevolence fund at church a time or two. She's the only one, though, who's ever made sure to give back the money even when told not to."

"Pride and compassion," Maggie said.

"Pride and hope," Jared reminded. "Romans 12:12, remember?" He tightened his fingers on her shoulder and this time she looked up at him in a way that gave him hope.

"Dad, we need to leave," Ryan encouraged. "I want to go home."

"You never want to go home."

"I do today." It didn't escape Jared's notice that his oldest son was looking at Maggie while he asked.

As everyone began putting on their winter apparel, a cab pulled up in front of the shop.

Jared had been helping Maggie as she put jackets back on soft hangers and carefully attached the bow ties to each collar. She turned, saw the cab and nearly sat down on the chair containing Billy's top hat.

"Someone you know?" Jared guessed.

"My mother-in-law."

Chapter Sixteen

Kelly Tate took in the crowded room, the cluttered stairs leading up to the apartment and calmly said, "Where shall I have him put my luggage?"

"Upstairs."

Instead of the cabbie, who'd never before driven his cab from Des Moines to Roanoke, the McCreedy men carried in the luggage. It went upstairs and into the bedroom Maggie shared with Cassidy.

Maggie would be sleeping on the couch tonight.

Everyone introduced themselves to Kelly, chattered about the wedding and about the Christmas thief, and then—too soon—started to leave. Joel and Beth were first. They were going on a wedding cake hunt. Billy and Jared took a moment to look at the window over Maggie's kitchen table.

"Needs replacing," Billy said.

"I'm getting good at windows," Jared said, taking a tape measure out of his back pocket.

"You carry tape measures with you?" Maggie asked.

"Not usually, but I remembered what Henry said the other night."

"Henry?" Kelly asked.

"He owns the shop across the street," Maggie answered, "and I'm not ready for a new window yet."

Once everyone left, Maggie showed Kelly the shop, mentioning the tree and what was missing and pointing out the mural Beth was working on.

"I didn't know you did weddings," Kelly said.

"I don't, usually. She's doing vintage, so we found the men's tuxes online. We found one of the bridesmaid's dresses and then I made the second. Beth borrowed the wedding dress from a friend."

"She doesn't like it."

"Huh?"

"Beth. She's not crazy about the dress."

Maggie blinked. Kelly had been here all of thirty minutes and already had an opinion that Maggie needed to pay attention to.

"What makes you think that?"

"Her sisters…"

"Susan and Linda."

"They kept looking in the mirror on your door. They couldn't stop looking. Beth glanced at it a couple times and then took off her dress."

"I like the dress, Grandma." Cassidy pranced from one side of the room to the other. "Did you see Matt? He's the second biggest boy. Isn't he cute? And Caleb, too. They have horses and a dog and—"

"And almost all the things on your Christmas list," Maggie finished.

Cassidy nodded. "Except for red cowboy boots. Matt says red's a silly color for cowboy boots but Caleb thinks they'll be cool."

Maggie hadn't seen Cassidy's Christmas list in a few days, but Cassidy knew right where it was and fetched it. Knowing how small their apartment was and sensing that toys weren't going to flow down the chimney in unlimited numbers, Cassidy had kept her list small. After Thanksgiving, Maggie had suggested five items. Cassidy immediately wrote down two: red cowboy boots and a puppy. Of course, Maggie knew the list had grown. She'd seen the request for a baby brother. She'd heard about the addition of the horse.

"I'm at five now," Cassidy said proudly. "Mom says five is a reasonable number."

Kelly took the list. "Red cowboy boots, puppy, baby brother, horse, and," her voice faltered, "a daddy."

"Oh, my," said Maggie.

"Oh, my, indeed," said Kelly.

Kelly took Cassidy shopping. Since four of the items on the Santa list needed negotiating, Kelly felt the task necessary. The moment the door shut behind them, Maggie collapsed on her stool.

Without warning, her mother-in-law had decided to deliver the red cowboy boots in person and to stick around until after Christmas. At the moment, Maggie had no idea if the size of the apartment had changed Kelly's mind about staying. Based on how happy Kelly was to see Cassidy the answer was no.

Just wait until Kelly opened the refrigerator and saw how little food there was. Just wait until she saw the size of the shower in the minuscule bathroom. Just wait until Kelly heard that Cassidy had already picked out who she wanted for her next father.

There'd been a picture next to the words *a daddy*. Kelly might not have recognized the baseball cap and brown parka, but Maggie had. Cassidy had picked out Jared McCreedy.

Based on Thursday's lunch, he was willing to think about it.

Maggie let out a breath and looked up. The decorative tin ceiling was one of her favorite things about the shop. It was in great shape and even came complete with trim and borders. It had sheltered a hundred years of shop owners and their problems.

No, not it. God, really. He was in the little town and its people. He was with every person Maggie came in contact with lately. Everyone except Maggie.

"Thank You," Maggie mouthed then immediately felt guilty. Who was she thanking? No one. Because she didn't pray. Not even to say thank-you.

Things had been happening fast and furious since Thanksgiving, and really, she'd not had a chance to do anything but react.

"And if I prayed, I'd be praying right now."

Saturdays were usually the busiest day of the week, and today was no exception. As one customer after another came in the shop, some to buy and others to talk about tonight's meeting, Maggie was grateful for their patronage. Because she'd been tempted to pray and had she started, she might never have stopped.

Kelly and Cassidy came home with enough packages to require two trips up the stairs. They'd done the town and had even met Hillary at the Red Barn Grille.

"I've never seen her so happy," Kelly said, nodding at Cassidy. "We ran into at least three friends of hers from school. Then, all the men from that wedding party were at the restaurant."

"They bought our lunch," Cassidy said.

"We're going to put this stuff away and then go to the library. Cassidy says you both have overdue books."

Maggie almost fell off her stool. "Yes, we do. Cassidy, why didn't you remind me?"

"We've been busy, but Grandma has time to take me."

"I'm looking forward to it."

A customer came in, then another and another. Maggie started breathing a little easier. If she could keep this up, she'd have enough for a decent Christmas dinner. Kelly was a great cook, too.

Kelly and Cassidy came back down the stairs. Cassidy held on to her grandma's hand until she got to the bottom. She could see Henry shoveling his sidewalk across the street. "I've got to tell Henry that Grandma's here," Cassidy shouted. She turned to Kelly and asked, "Want to come with me?"

"I'll be over in just a minute."

"Look both ways before you cross the street," Maggie reminded.

Kelly, no stranger to winter, had on a fur coat, tights and knee boots. She walked over and looked in the pile Maggie was ringing up.

"Great Nehru jacket," she said. "Looks like it's actually from the 1960s."

"It is," Maggie affirmed.

The customer said something about making sure to come back and then Kelly and Maggie were alone. They both looked out the window and across the street where Cassidy had taken over the shovel and Henry sat on a bench both advising and listening to her.

"I see why you like it here," Kelly said.

"Yeah, it's a pretty special place."

"He's wearing a brown parka," Kelly observed of Henry. "But I'm thinking he's not the man Cassidy was drawing on her Christmas list."

"No, he's not."

"Are you dating Jared McCreedy?" Kelly asked bluntly.

"No."

"Does he want to date you?"

"Yes."

"Then, what's wrong?"

Maggie's throat tightened. No way could she tell Kelly

why she wasn't free to date a good man like Jared. Kelly wouldn't understand. Kelly wouldn't forgive.

Maggie didn't forgive herself.

Bob's Hardware Store carried plenty of windows. Jared paced back and forth trying to decide whether to keep Maggie's words in mind.

She'd said she wasn't ready for a new window. Meaning, she couldn't afford one right now. However, she needed a window. Not only was moisture a sign that cold air was getting it, but soon she'd have mold and decay.

If she didn't already.

He hated thinking about her up in that apartment, silent and cold.

Common sense told him the window could wait a month or two until they'd either entered a friendship, and he'd advise her; or they'd entered a relationship, and he could just do what he did best: take care of things.

She was too prickly now for him to buy and install without permission even though his gut told him that she needed a new window as a Christmas present more than she needed flowers or a candle.

"Not romantic enough," was Billy's input before heading off to the section stocked with kitchen supplies.

"You need a window?" Bob asked the obvious.

"Three foot tall by four foot wide."

"I've got Anderson, Pella and Marvin all in stock and in that size. Wait, I sold the last Anderson two weeks ago. Kyle Totwell's putting that old farm back together piece by piece."

"That he is," Jared said. "I helped him install his window. Why don't you go ahead and put together a price for me on both the Pella and Marvin. Let me know what I'll need and how much it is."

"I'll email it to you by Monday," Bob promised. "You going to the church tonight?"

"Wouldn't miss it."

Jared had already done what he could. They'd gone to the Red Barn Grille for lunch. No doubt, Hillary's tips were up, but that only solved one problem.

There were still two weeks until Christmas and whoever was committing the crimes was getting braver.

What if Maggie had been home when her place had been struck?

The Main Street Church was almost full when Maggie, Cassidy and Kelly walked in. Maggie wanted to slink in and find a spot in the back. Not Cassidy. She spotted Matt and took off like a magnet. Kelly wasn't far behind. Maggie didn't have much of a choice.

Next thing she knew she was in a full pew and sitting so close to Jared that her coat was unnecessary. Somebody had turned up the heat, or at least that's what Maggie hoped. Surely it couldn't be Jared's effect on her.

Kelly wound up next to Billy Staples. Maggie could see why Grandpa Billy was held in such high esteem. He had Caleb on one side with a dozen action movie figures doing battle.

"Are they saving the church?" Kelly asked Caleb.

"Maybe," Caleb answered.

Both Matt and Cassidy had taken notepaper from the back of the pew in front of them and were busy drawing. Matt had a near perfect Santa flying around the world. Cassidy had an all-pencil Santa who was more beard than belly.

Kelly and Billy chuckled companionably. Even though Jared separated her from her mother-in-law, Maggie could hear part of the conversation.

"I've been to Manhattan a time or two," Billy was telling Kelly. "It's been a while, though. I saw *42nd Street* back in the eighties. Jerry Orbach played Julian Marsh."

"I saw that one," Kelly breathed. "I was with my new husband. Dan wasn't born yet."

"I've often thought," Billy confided, "if I could do it all over, I'd act."

Both Joel and Jared's mouths dropped open.

"Your mother-in-law's nicer than I envisioned," Jared whispered.

"I'm not sure who this lady is," Maggie whispered back. "I think she's taken over Kelly's body. Be scared. Be very, very scared."

Mike Russell, who looked very much like a preacher even in jeans instead of his Sunday suit, took his place behind the podium. Alex Farraday stood, in full uniform, next to him. The auditorium's buzz increased instead of decreased. Tensions were high. Maggie used the time to look around. She had a vested interest in how tonight turned out. So did the minister. Jared pointed to his neighbors, the McClanahans. They'd been hit early on. "I don't see the Totwells," he whispered in Maggie's ear.

"I called them," Billy whispered back. "They said they'd try to make it. Their little boy's got a bad cold."

"Lisa had it earlier this week," Cassidy said. "She kept sneezing on me."

"Thanks for coming," the minister said loudly into the mike. "Let's go ahead and start with a prayer."

For once, Maggie wasn't the only one who didn't bow. But she listened to every word and felt the stirrings of something akin to comfort.

Hard to believe since Kelly Tate sat a few feet away.

"I'm Mike Russell, preacher here at the Main Street Church. Tonight we're going to hear some hard facts from the chief of police. We're also going to put our heads together and see if we can't figure out how to stop anyone else from losing their Christmas."

"We need more police," someone shouted.

Someone else said, "We need to watch the interstate. It has to be someone from out of town."

Mike moved aside and let Alex take the podium. "We don't think it's someone from the outside. In every instance the home owner was gone and people knew they'd be gone, whether it be for a church, school or work responsibility."

"That's right," the minister said. "I was here at church. At the same time, Hillary Phillips was at the restaurant and her two children were at the babysitter, like they are every Friday night."

"Not one of the break-ins appears random," Alex continued. "Plus, as most of you figured out already, the thief is targeting families and making off with toys while leaving items more valuable behind."

"Unless they happen to be easy to take and convenient," the minister added.

"Yes," Alex agreed. "What we want is for the community to band together. If you're going to be gone, ask a neighbor to keep an eye out. If there's a car in the neighborhood, even if it belongs to someone you know, write down the license number. That way we can see if there's a vehicle that happens to be in the area each and every time a theft occurs."

"We'll pray for whoever is taking our things, but we need to catch them and help them first."

"I'll help them," someone muttered in the back. "I'll help them right to jail."

Most people smiled and halfheartedly nodded. Down Maggie's pew, she could see Beth, a little white-faced. Maggie didn't know the whole story. She just knew that at one time Beth's mom had been the school secretary and that she'd embezzled for years in order to send her girls to college.

Looking at Kelly, Maggie realized she wouldn't need to do that. If it were for Cassidy, Kelly would be at the ready, checkbook open and pen in hand.

Maggie didn't want that much help. But she also didn't understand Beth's mother's choice.

Alex continued, "Please be sure to lock all doors and windows. Don't let anything valuable be seen from the windows, and yes, that might mean moving your Christmas tree. If you have time, go ahead and walk your neighborhoods. If you see anything suspicious, anything at all, give the police a call."

A few men went up and down the aisles and passed out papers. Maggie soon held a map of Roanoke. There were stars wherever a theft had taken place. No one area seemed targeted.

"Now that the police have done their thing," Mike Russell said, taking back the podium, "it's time for the church to step in. I've looked at the stars on this map. At least a third of the places hit belong to single parents."

"And single grandparents," Henry said loudly. "Don't forget your train."

"I won't," Michael promised. "There's not much time, but in the spirit of Christmas, the church would like to do something, maybe a quick donation or fundraiser."

The mood switched. Not everyone in the room was a church member. The word *donation* sent off a bit of a ripple throughout the crowd.

"What kind of donation?"

"I don't know," Michael said, "Maybe five dollars a family."

"What kind of fundraiser were you thinking?" Joel asked. "Something here at the church?"

"Could be."

"What did we do with the money from our winter program?" Henry asked.

"It went to the mission field, already mailed. How many would come to a second program if we could scramble and put it together?"

Caleb and Cassidy were among the few who raised their hands.

A woman up front raised her hand. Michael quieted the audience. She stood and turned around. "We just bought the Carver place this past summer."

Maggie recognized her. She'd been in Hand Me Ups Thursday.

"I normally wouldn't speak up, but my daughter and I were talking about this on the way here. See, we went to Solitaire Farm over Thanksgiving and went through that maze. We thought they'd do it for Christmas and drove all the way out there last week. It's just an idea, but I'd pay upward to twenty dollars if they did it up on a Christmas theme."

"That's an idea!" Michael said. "Jared, Billy, Joel, what do you think?"

Joel was already nodding, but Maggie noticed Billy and Jared exchange looks.

"All this and a wedding," Billy murmured.

"We'll divide the proceeds between the families who need it most," Michael said.

"Come on, Jared," a man Maggie didn't recognize said. "We'll help you organize the maze and even donate more hay if you need it."

"McClanahan," Jared barbed, "you're real good about volunteering when it isn't your home."

"Hey, I get the traffic going to your place. Sometimes it even leaves the road and hits my fence."

"Once," Joel said. "It only happened once and I fixed the fence, remember."

"We've got the wedding," Jared said, "and we don't have anything to give people."

"Like what?" Kelly asked.

Beth had obviously been thinking. "Hot chocolate and baked goods. The church will help with the baked goods."

"I bake," Kelly said. "Just give me an oven."

Maggie doubted Kelly had seen the size of the oven in her apartment.

"When can you do it?" Michael asked.

"Next Friday," Joel volunteered.

"The day after the Christmas play at school." Billy now looked pale whereas Beth had gotten her color back.

"We'll string Christmas lights," Joel said.

"We'll use all the empty presents that I've wrapped," Beth add.

Caleb pulled on Billy's sleeve. "And you can be Santa."

"What!"

Kelly agreed, "You said you wished you could act. Here's your chance."

In front of the audience, Michael Russell said, "Let's pray."

Jared bowed his head. He nodded as he did it. And as he nodded, he looked at Maggie and took her hand. She knew he was thinking about her, helping her. She loved the way his hand felt, the roughness, the strength.

The window would have been easier.

Chapter Seventeen

It was late when Maggie put on her pajamas and put Cassidy to bed. She cleared off her side, getting it ready for Kelly, and wished she'd thought to change the sheets.

"I would have gotten a motel room but I couldn't bear the thought of being alone in a strange town," Kelly said. "I'm sleeping on the couch, you know that, right?"

"I want to sleep with Grandma," Cassidy murmured, half asleep and turning to face them.

"Guess that solves the problem," Maggie said. "You're the chosen one."

"No, I'll take the couch. It won't be the first time. Plus, I always get up early."

"So do I."

"I insist."

"It's my house," Maggie said.

"But—"

"My house," Maggie reminded, "and you're always welcome here as long as you're easy to get along with."

Kelly's lips twitched, and she paused before saying, "I appreciate that. I think. I'll just get my pajamas on real quick."

Knowing that Kelly liked a cup of tea before bed, Maggie put on the water. She had tea, purchased by habit because of the months she'd lived with Kelly. While the water boiled, she turned the couch into a bed and, after checking on Cassidy, turned the television on low. An old Christmas movie with Jimmy Stewart played.

After the water boiled, Maggie brought Kelly her tea and settled into the easy chair right next to the sofa. She had her own cup of tea, too. It must be a mood thing. Picking up the box of elf hat material, Maggie started on yet one more.

"Do you have another needle?"

"Do birds sing?"

Over an hour later, they finished the last of the elf hats and made a couple extras for the maze.

"Why didn't we ever sit and visit like this when I was living with you?" Maggie asked.

"You were grieving, and I had my friends and meetings. We were too busy to enjoy each other. Plus, we were both angry. Not at each other, but at fate. A parent should not outlive her child. And, believe me, I know the void left when a husband dies. Now, tell me about your business and finances and young man. Don't leave anything out."

Maggie almost laughed. Who'd have guessed that telling her mother-in-law about Hand Me Ups business and finances would be easier than telling her about a male friend?

That's all Jared was: a friend.

It was time for bed. Joel took care of Matt, telling him all about his and Beth's plans come next week and how Matt could help. At a time when Matt had needed a friend, Beth had been there. They had a special relationship that extended to include Joel. Billy tackled Caleb, literally. Then, in respect to Billy's back, Joel carried Caleb up the stairs and into the bath.

By the time Jared put away the last of the popcorn dishes and turned off the kitchen light, Ryan was already in his room, under the covers, playing his handheld game.

Stepping over clothes and some sports equipment, Jared made his way to the twin bed and sat down on the edge.

"I don't need to be tucked in," Ryan said, putting his game on the nightstand, turning so he faced the wall, and closing his eyes.

"Everyone needs to be tucked in."

Ryan turned his head frowned. "Are you going to talk to me about Maggie?"

"Why do you think that?"

"Last time you came in for a man-to-man talk was when I bumped into a girl at church and almost knocked her down. You said I had to apologize and be nice. You seem to come in the most when it has to do with girls."

Had it been that long? And was that the only reason? Usually, Jared was so busy making sure Caleb was in bed.

"I check on you every night."

"Not while I'm awake."

"You're right," Jared acknowledged. "I'll do better."

Ryan rolled over and faced his father. "So, are you here to talk about Maggie?"

"Yes."

"Great, just great." Typical nine-year-old, Ryan knew that tone was everything.

"Yes, it might be," Jared agreed. "But, then again, she and I might just be friends. Either way, you need to respect her."

"I don't want another mother. I liked the one I had."

"I liked the wife I had, too. When your mother died, I felt like someone took a scythe and cut my legs off at the knees. Sometimes it hurt to breathe, to walk, to try to go on."

Ryan turned so his face was in the pillow.

"We have it good here. I know," Jared said. "But, it could be better, and change is coming whether you want it or not. Another few weeks and Beth will be living here."

"I like Beth. I know her."

"Nothing's going to happen too fast or without you being

part of the decision making. But, if Maggie lets me, I intend on asking her out again and again."

"Ew."

"Ew?"

"She's such a girly girl." Ryan sounded so much like an authority that Jared almost laughed. But, now was not the time. Reaching under the covers, Jared found Ryan's hand and held it. "From the time we brought you home, I've valued you, loved you and wanted what was best for you. You have to trust me now."

"I trust you."

Still holding on to his son's hand, Jared said a prayer. "Father, help me do a better job each day of being a father to my sons, a worker in my fields and a giver at our church. Guide us all in our decisions. Amen."

Ryan didn't say anything, and Jared stood and retucked the quilt around his son's frame. Then, he went to the door and turned off the light. He'd already mostly shut the door behind him when he heard a soft, "I love you, Dad."

Ryan would be all right. It might take a while, but Ryan was really the one who remembered Mandy the most. No wonder he was scared.

Jared was scared, too.

Scared that he was falling in love with a woman who couldn't, wouldn't, love him back no matter how hard he prayed.

Kelly took Cassidy to church Sunday morning, casting a disappointed look in Maggie's direction. "It's past time," she said. For the second Sunday in a row, Maggie cleaned the apartment.

On Monday, Kelly worked in the shop, helping customers and baking while Maggie finished the costumes for Thursday's school program. A couple times Kelly started making suggestions, about a certain price, about the mural, or about

the store's arrangement, but just a look from Maggie stilled
any discussion about doing it Kelly's way. By the end of the
day, Hand Me Ups smelled more like a bakery than a vintage clothes shop.

On Tuesday, right before lunchtime, Jared showed up at
the door. He smiled at Kelly, making Maggie wonder what
they'd talked about Sunday morning at church. Kelly simply
handed him a cookie. She'd been giving them out to customers, too, and sales were up.

Maggie had gone two days without seeing Jared. She'd
parted company with him after the town meeting, about nine
Saturday night, and now here it was eleven Tuesday morning.

Sixty-two hours.

Not that she'd been counting.

"Tonight," he asked, "would you like to drive around town
and look at the Christmas lights?"

"I'll watch Cassidy," Kelly volunteered quickly.

"Oh, she'd like to come along—" Maggie started to say,
and then she saw the expression in Jared's eye. He was asking her out on a date, a real honest-to-goodness date. Even
though she'd told him straight out that she didn't belong anywhere near his heart or prayers.

Maggie looked at Kelly. She simply nodded and mouthed,
"Go."

"I don't…"

Saying no was safe. Maggie could concentrate on keeping
the store running, on keeping Cassidy running, on keeping
hold of the precious control she needed in life.

Saying yes was chancy. Life had been a little out of control ever since Jared had appeared that awkward morning
and cleaned up pancake batter spilled in her tiny kitchen.
Seemed that since then, he'd been around so much she'd
gotten used to him.

"Ahem," Kelly said, back to being the impatient mother-in-law. "You need to finish your answer. I suggest you say, 'I don't have any other plans and would love to.'"

"I'm sorry, Jared. My mother-in-law's here visiting, and I've got a lot of work to do. Maybe another time."

Jared nodded, his smile not diminishing a bit. "I'll ask again. For now, I'm back to the school and finishing up the stage. You'll be around later for practice, right?"

"Yeeess."

"Good, I look forward to seeing you."

He walked out the door and Maggie turned to Kelly. "I can't believe you're encouraging me to go out with him. Do you know how hard it is to tell him no?"

"And I can't believe you need encouragement. And why on earth would you tell him no? He's a good man who happens to be falling in love with you. He's the kind of man who'll take on Cassidy as his own. Maybe you'll even have more children. You're only twenty-seven. Life doesn't end just because a spouse dies."

"You never remarried," Maggie pointed out.

The last customer left, without buying anything, and Kelly walked to the door and turned the sign to Closed. Maggie let out a tiny protest.

"Five minutes," Kelly promised. "I just need five minutes to slap some sense into you."

To Maggie's amazement, the moment Kelly turned from locking the door, she burst into tears. Awkwardly, Maggie drew her mother-in-law into a hug noticing how ramrod straight she remained and how tense she was. They'd never done more than the get-close-and-pat-each-other-on-the-back kind of hug.

"If you're going to slap some sense into me, you'd better stop crying," Maggie advised.

"I'm so glad I came," Kelly blubbered.

"So that you can slap some sense into me?"

"No, so that I can stop thinking that my way is best, stop

pressuring you to come back to Manhattan, and start realizing that my granddaughter can bloom without me."

"Okay, well, then I'm glad you came, too."

Almost as quickly as it started, Kelly's tears stopped. "I need a cup of tea," she said. "Give me a moment." Up the stairs she went. Maggie glanced at the Closed sign on the door, adjusted a few clothes racks, and followed her mother-in-law up the stairs.

The window by the kitchen table was frosted over. Kelly drew a tiny circle on it with her finger and looked out. "You're a really good mother," she said.

"What?" A comment about parenting skills was not what Maggie expected.

"You know enough to let her have wings. That was my problem with Dan. Because we had just one, I wanted to enjoy every moment and forgot that my son needed to enjoy every moment, too."

"You were a good parent. Dan turned out just fine."

"Dan couldn't wait to get away from home. That's why he joined the military."

Maggie wasn't going to lie because that's exactly what happened, but… "You did the best you knew how."

"You want to know why I didn't get remarried?" Kelly asked. "And, believe me, I had plenty of opportunities."

"Why?"

Kelly leaned in. "I never remarried because I wasn't willing to share Dan with another man. I wanted all control, and I got it. But the cost was high. In the end, the only thing I had control over was myself."

Control had always been an issue in Maggie's life, first battling her father who didn't understand a girl's needs, and then battling Dan over Cassidy's needs, and now maintaining control when there was no father or Dan in sight.

Well, Jared was in sight.

She'd given up a bit of control the day of the break-in. That little bit was like a door opening and letting Maggie see the potential in the world, potential being Henry Throxmorton who'd come across the street to help. Jared McCreedy who'd installed a new lock on her door within an hour. Alex Farraday who'd stopped by or called at least once a day with updates.

And now control was giving over, just a bit, to Kelly Tate who was turning out to be a natural storekeeper who gave cookies to customers and talked them into buying things they didn't need.

When Maggie didn't answer, Kelly said, "Really, the only one who should be in control is God. How I wished I'd understood that when Dan was young."

Oh, yeah, and God had been in control when Dan died.

That's what Maggie couldn't forget.

"I'm madder than spit," Beth said, holding a Christmas tree in place while Jared secured the bottom. Only two days until the Roanoke Elementary Christmas program and just about everything was in place.

"He forgot. That's all."

"Joel never forgets when it comes to his precious rodeo, and now we're doing all the work."

Jared stood, stretching his back. He'd placed a dozen tiny fake trees, donated by Bob's Hardware, around the school's gymnasium. Right now, the older grades were putting out folding chairs. On stage, the kindergartners were practicing their song. Caleb's voice was loudest of all, which might be okay if he were singing the same song. Jared wasn't quite sure.

"We'll get the maze done, even without him. The McClanahans have been out every night."

"And my mother-in-law has made a thousand cookies." Maggie stepped up behind Beth. "We'll be coming on Friday after school to help."

"Friday's going to be ridiculously busy, and we'll be tired after Thursday night's program."

Beth walked away, shaking her head.

"It's not the maze that's bothering her," Maggie said. "It's that she's getting married in a little over two weeks and there's so much to do."

"And so little time to do it," Jared agreed. "I told them a Christmas wedding would be tough. Hey, I have something for you."

Reaching in his back pocket, he pulled out some papers. "I priced a new window for your apartment. Here are two cost comparisons. When Joel gets back in town, we'll do the work so you don't need to worry about labor."

"I'll pay for labor."

"Nah, putting in a window is easy, and we're pros. Remember, we did it at the Totwells'. Plus, you can give me some more advice about Caleb."

"Advice is free. Only with my mother-in-law does it come with a price."

"She seems fairly harmless."

"It's been an amazing visit so far," Maggie admitted, shrugging out of her coat and laying it on a chair. "When she first showed up, I just…"

"Just what?"

In a much quieter voice, Maggie said, "I wished she'd go away."

"We all wish our problems away at one time or another. By the way, speaking about problems, the allergy pediatrician called me yesterday," Jared said. "They think he's allergic to milk. All those questionnaires I filled out finally made sense to somebody. Caleb's complained about stomachaches since I can remember. We have to go back for more tests but, for the moment, the doctors are thinking it might be milk, eggs and cheese more than ADD."

Maggie shook her head. "And you're a farmer with an abundance of milk, eggs and cheese."

"I've got an abundance of a lot of things, and I'm always willing to share them with the right person."

"Jared, don't."

"Why, Maggie? Is it because it's Christmas and you're thinking about your late husband?"

"I need to go up on stage and check the costumes, see if they're in good condition. Kids tend to be rough during rehearsals."

"I'm a patient man. I didn't used to think so. But, thanks to you, I've learned quite a bit." He threw her words, from so many weeks ago, back at her. "Patience is a virtue, have it if you can. Seldom found in a woman. Never in a man."

Maggie looked away.

"Never in a man," he nudged gently. "Just give me a bit of hope. That's all I ask."

"It wouldn't be fair. You deserve someone—"

"I'm picky," Jared interrupted. "It's taken me a long time to find the person I want. I mean, deserve."

Before Maggie could answer, Beth came back, holding her cell phone for Jared to take. "It's Joel. He's got a few things to say, and I'm not talking to him."

"Hello, bro," Jared said. "I see I need to give marital counsel even before you're married."

"I'm half tempted to pack up and come home," Joel admitted. "I'm not in the mood to ride, and that never goes well. But I've paid the entry free."

"Yes." Jared looked at Beth. "The entry fee is nonrefundable. I can see why you feel torn."

"Look," Joel said. "Can you make it over to Freeport today? Remember Jerry, the kid who wanted to be a bull rider and his dad owns Binky Burgers?"

Only Joel would throw that much information at Jared and think he might possibly remember. "No."

"Well, they've got a Santa sled they put in front of the fast-food restaurant every December. They're going to let us borrow it for Saturday night seeing as how it's a good cause. But, someone needs to go get it."

"That's perfect!"

"What?" said Beth. "What's perfect?"

"He found us a Santa sled to use Saturday night."

"Hmm, long-distance help still means we do the work," she sniffed.

"I heard that," Joel said. "Tell her I'll be back late Sunday and that I love her."

Jared relayed the message.

"Tell him," Beth said, "that he can stay gone."

Jared started to relay the message, but realized almost immediately that the only thing keeping Maggie upright was his hand under her arm. She looked about to faint.

"What's wrong with—" he started to say.

"Maggie, are you all right?" Beth asked.

Shaking her head, Maggie ran from the room, out the door, and to her car.

Without her coat.

It wasn't so much the coat that had Jared most worried, it was the words she flung back at Beth.

"Don't say that," she told Beth. "Don't ever say that."

Jared watched Maggie's ashen face as she jerked her vehicle into reverse and left the parking lot.

Beside him, Beth stood all confused. "What just happened? What did I say?"

"I don't know," Jared answered. "But whatever it was, you struck a nerve."

Beth thought for a moment. "I told you to tell Joel to stay gone."

Jared nodded.

"That must have been it. Me telling Joel to stay gone."

Jared agreed. Those words had Maggie looking like she'd seen a ghost, and from her words, Jared guessed she'd been haunted for a long time.

Chapter Eighteen

Beth couldn't leave. She had twenty-five singing kindergartners on stage. Jared didn't have such a dilemma. He was in his truck and on the lookout for Maggie within a minute.

What had just happened?

Don't say that, she'd told Beth. *Don't ever say that.*

What exactly had Beth said?

Tell him that he can stay gone.

Well, at least now Jared had some idea what was bothering Maggie, but not enough idea for him to do anything but gnaw at it.

He went to Maggie's shop. She wasn't there, but Kelly promised to call the minute she turned up. Her car wasn't at the library, the post office or the church.

Driving down Main Street, Jared saw one vehicle after another that he recognized, but not Maggie's van.

At Bob's Hardware, he watched as Kyle Totwell carried something to his truck. Kyle waved as he climbed in the driver's side.

Click.

Something flashed in Jared's brain. The window aisle. Bob saying they'd sold the last of the Anderson three-by-fours two weeks ago. The old screwdriver in the door and

Kyle Totwell talking about his grandfather leaving him everything, everything old.

Great, just great.

Jared pulled out his cell phone and called Chief Alex Farraday.

"I'm in my truck and don't like using the cell. Do me a favor. Call Bob's Hardware and asked Bob when he sold Kyle Totwell the Anderson window."

Alex didn't hesitate, just said, "Will do," and hung up. A minute later, he returned the call. "December first."

"When did Kyle say the thief broke the window getting into his living room to steal the presents?"

After a moment, Alex came back with, "December third."

"You do know," Jared asked, "that Joel and I helped him install the new window on December 5."

"He purchased the window before the thief broke the window," Jared and Alex said together.

"I hope I'm wrong," Jared said, thinking of the two children and the woman who'd loaned Beth her wedding dress. Chances were she didn't know what Kyle had been up to.

It would be even worse if she did.

Right after Jared ended the call to Alex, Kelly Tate called. "Maggie stopped by. She's heading back to the school. She says she's got commitments to keep. She's been crying. You know anything about that?"

"I'll tell you when I figure it out," Jared promised.

Back at the school, however, Maggie became an expert at avoidance, and Jared didn't know how to approach her. But, the good thing about small towns was, she couldn't avoid him forever.

"Someone's ringing the doorbell," Kelly said.

"I'll get it," Cassidy offered. Because of the Christmas program and all, homework was not an issue this Tuesday night. The teachers were too busy to assign it.

"It's probably Beth wanting to talk again," Maggie said.

"She's your best friend. You need to talk to her," Kelly advised.

"I will, just not today."

"Then talk to me."

Maggie shook her head. Not a chance, not a chance.

Opening the window, she peered down at Jared McCreedy. He held some presents in his arms. For a moment, the only emotion Maggie felt was annoyance. He'd brought her presents. She'd told him time and time again she wasn't interested.

Then, she recognized her own wrapping paper.

"You found Cassidy's presents!" she shouted down. For a moment happiness took over, pushing aside the guilt she'd been feeling.

"We found everything. Let me in."

Cassidy and Kelly were at her heels as she went down the stairs. Maggie opened the door and Jared breezed in. He gave the presents to Cassidy. "I believe these are yours."

In response, Cassidy ran upstairs to put them under the tree.

Maggie's jewelry was in a sack. She opened it, checked the items and smiled. "I don't care about the jewelry, but the presents are greatly appreciated." She turned to Kelly. "Counting the red cowboy boots you bought her, she'll now have three pairs."

"Every girls needs a closetful of shoes," Kelly responded.

"Usually the police keep evidence, but with the evidence being Christmas presents and the thief confessing to everything, Alex decided that the good book had the best advice."

"What's that?" Maggie asked. "Thou shalt not steal?"

"Let the thief no longer steal," Kelly quoted from memory, "but rather let him labor, doing honest work with his own hands, so that he may have something to share with anyone in need."

"I think," Jared said, "that Alex was thinking more along the lines of 'Give and it will be given unto you.'"

"They all work." Kelly took a few steps up the stairs. "I'll check on Cassidy."

Maggie knew exactly what her mother-in-law was doing. She was leaving Maggie with Jared so they could talk.

"Who was the thief?"

"Kyle Totwell. He couldn't afford to buy gifts for his wife's family and he was ashamed. Apparently the first crime was spur of the moment. He saw an open door and an opportunity. I guess when Alex drove up the lane to their farm, Kyle started crying like a baby."

"What's going to happen to him?"

"I don't know. Everything was there, so the presents will be returned to their rightful owners and in time for Christmas. That will count as something."

"I'm glad for the other families. It was a worry." Maggie stepped to the door, reaching for the knob. "Are you going to cancel the maze now?"

"No, we've advertised it from Freeport to Des Moines. Even if I tried to cancel it, people would show up. I don't want to have to tell a hundred people they drove all the way out to Solitaire Farm for nothing."

"Kelly's baked again all day. She's also working on your Santa suit."

Jared rolled his eyes. "I can't believe Billy's back chose to go out now. The church has one, you know. I'll just wear it."

"Hmm, then I'm not sure what she's working on. It's red, white-fur lined, and she says it's for you."

Jared stepped toward the door, closer to her and bent his head. "There's still time to drive around tonight and look at the lights."

"No."

"You can tell me why you got upset today. After all, it's your fault we stumbled on to what Kyle Totwell was doing."

"What?"

"I was hunting for you when I put two and two together about the window he'd purchased." Quickly, Jared filled her in on the details.

When he finished, she still shook her head no. "I've got Kelly here and it's almost time to put Cassidy to bed."

"I can take care of myself," Kelly hollered from upstairs, "and Cassidy just put herself to bed!"

"Did not," Cassidy said calmly.

"I'm going to keep asking you," Jared promised.

"And I'm going to keep saying no," Maggie replied.

Jared tussled the top of her head. "Good, I like a challenge.'

Thursday night, the Roanoke Elementary Christmas program was a success, even though Caleb sang the wrong song and Cassidy got tangled up in the giant Santa bag while handing out presents to her elves.

Matt was so busy helping her that he forgot to be shy and actually did his part.

Ryan got a standing ovation.

Friday, Maggie closed Hand Me Ups early and piled everyone into her van and headed out to Solitaire Farm. "I've never been out here," she said, handing Kelly directions.

"You're kidding."

"No. We didn't make it to the Thanksgiving maze, and there's just no reason to come out this way."

"I can think of plenty of reasons," Kelly said.

Forty minutes later, Maggie saw the number two reason to visit a place like Solitaire Farm. On the rural road was Solitaire's Market. It looked like an old-time log cabin. There were rocking chairs, with price tags, on the front porch. Giant windows offered a peek at what was inside. This was where Joel sold produce and goods. It was beautiful.

Trucks were parked by the maze, and people—Maggie

knew all of them—were stringing lights and putting up decorations.

"Wow," Cassidy said.

Maggie would need more than "wow" to describe what she saw next. The market didn't compare to the number one reason to visit Solitaire Farm. That would be the actual farm, past the trees, a good quarter mile down the gravel drive.

As dusk settled, lights glowed yellow in the windows. The farmhouse was white clapboard, two-storied and came with a wraparound front porch all draped in wintery white and dripping icicles. The yard went on forever, and a dog ran through the snow toward them.

"Captain Rex!" Cassidy shouted.

"What happened to normal names like Butch and Tiger?" Kelly asked.

As Maggie parked, Jared came to the porch and hurried down to open the van's door. Behind him came the others, all grabbing boxes of baked goods and helping in the ladies. The house was full of people.

The minister was wrapping presents. The McClanahans were lettering signs. Kelly headed right to the kitchen to stand alongside Billy as he decided which cookies would be served first and how much hot chocolate they'd need.

Beth was on the phone. "Everything's going fine. You be careful today. Don't get hurt. Go ahead and place."

She'd had time to retract her wish.

Jared took Maggie by the hand and led her in and out of rooms, up and down stairs, showing off his home. He pointed out the family portrait which included Mandy.

"She's beautiful," Maggie said, disengaging her hand.

"Yes, she was. And she would have liked you."

Last, he made her get back into her winter coat and took her out to the barn. "This is my favorite place."

There were three pens, each containing a horse. Hay bales were against one wall. A tractor took up most of the room.

"I come out here whenever I need to think. For a long time, after Mandy died, I came out here every evening for hours at a time. Lately, I've gone a whole week without coming here except for chores."

"That's good."

Someone shouted Jared's name and they headed back inside. Beth was busy giving people jobs for Saturday's maze day. Maggie wound up being assigned Solitaire Market duty. After all, people would be browsing both before and after their turn at the maze. There was no produce, but there were jars of honey, homemade soap and as Jared suggested, "Why don't you bring some of your shawls, mittens and stuff tomorrow to sell? We're in this together."

At seven, everyone gathered in the living room and Mike Russell, the minister, asked if there were any prayer requests before he offered thanks for the chili Billy and Kelly had whipped up. Soon, he had a list. He was praying for Tess Throxmorton's health. He was praying for winter to be over, for out-of-town travelers over the holidays, and especially—per Beth—for Joel's safety both on the bull and on the road.

Someone even suggested they pray for the Totwells. Every head, including Maggie's nodded. Soon, even though her eyes were open, she bowed her head.

"Father," the minister said, "we thank You for all You've done for us. Please be with those traveling over the holidays and those with health issues. We thank You for the McCreedys who've opened their home and land for good works. We pray that tomorrow night's activities will honor thy name. Amen."

Maggie settled on the bottom step of the stairs and looked around for Cassidy. She was in the kitchen with Billy and Kelly and the boys. Captain Rex was with them and helpfully lapped up the food that fell.

Jared soon nudged her over. "Room for me?"

There was nowhere else for him to sit, really.

"This is great. I love that we prayed for the Totwells."

"We prayed?" His smile widened.

Maggie tried to scoot over more, but there was no room. She was pressed right against him. She wasn't sure if she should be annoyed—and, really, being annoyed all the time was just bothersome—or just enjoy the contact. "Yes, I prayed."

"The Totwells have been on a lot of hearts today," Jared said. "Mike has been calling the people who had their presents stolen to see how much each of them needed from tonight's fundraiser. Very few needed any money. He started querying where our proceeds should go. Guess what we're doing with the lion's share of the money?"

"The church?"

"Not a cent."

"Salvation Army?"

"That was suggested. No, we're giving most of it to Sophia Totwell. With her husband in jail, she's going to need all the help she can get."

"Wow."

"It was Beth and Joel's idea."

"Because of Beth's mother," Maggie guessed.

"We all make mistakes. Nearly every family the preacher spoke with thought the same things."

Jared had no idea how true his words were and how they made Maggie feel. Words had gotten her into this mess.

"We invited the Totwells tonight, but Sophia couldn't bear to come. If it weren't for the farm, she'd go home to her parents. When Joel gets back, she'll do just that and he's going to stay there for a while. Then, after he and Beth get married, she'll stay there, too, until Kyle figures out what he's going to do."

"That's nice of them."

"Yes." Jared turned to Maggie. "What do you think I should do? Should I offer to sell Joel back his portion of the farm? After all, he runs the market and does much of the work."

"Does he want his portion back?"

"He wants to live here."

"But does he want his portion back? What does he want?"

Jared shook his head. "He doesn't want all this land. He wants just enough for the animals, a workshop for his craft and the market. He's not a farmer."

"Have you gotten him a wedding present yet?" Maggie asked.

"No."

"Well, he's your brother. Give him just enough for the animals, a workshop and the market."

"I can't make ends meet without proceeds from the market."

"He gets the market, but you get to sell produce in it, too. After all, it's on your land."

Jared looked around the room until he spotted Beth. She, of course, was on the phone. "You talking to Joel?"

She nodded, and soon Jared was talking to Joel and Beth was sitting next to Maggie.

"Are you okay?" Beth asked.

"I'm fine. Sorry I wigged out on you the other day."

"It's the Christmas season." Beth wrapped her arm around Maggie. "It's hard on those of us who've suffered loss in the last year."

If just loss were the only thing Maggie suffered. In some ways, loss was easier than guilt.

Jared usually woke up before the alarm but not this Saturday. There'd been cleanup last night and excited kids and even an excited Billy.

"That woman knows how to bake a cookie," Billy said about Kelly.

"We all have our gifts," Jared agreed.

After breakfast, Billy and the boys got into the van and went out to put up signs pointing the way to the Christmas maze. Jared took care of the animals and general maintenance before heading to Solitaire's Market to make sure all was well there.

It was.

His next job was to start taking tables out of storage and put them where the lines would be.

Hot chocolate was fifty cents a cup. Cookies a dollar for two. There were also the usual cakes and brownies and such. The people from the Main Street Church and even a few non-church people had stepped up to the plate.

At five, helpers started arriving.

Jared only had eyes for one and she was taking her sweet time it looked like. Maggie Tate was always late. And he was quite willing to wait.

"She'll be here," Billy said.

At six, Jared went in to put on the Santa suit. "Really, Billy, you should be Santa."

"I can't take the weight of all those children. You know that."

"Then the minister."

"He'll be busy being the photographer and spreading the word while he does it. What an opportunity tonight is for him."

Looking in the mirror, Jared could only shake his head. He was too thin to look like the real thing. Plus, his dark hair showed through the scraggly white hair of the church's Santa suit. It had been worn often and Jared wished he'd have asked Billy to throw it in the wash. Too late now.

Maggie's van finally pulled in the driveway. He hurried to help her with the clothes and stuff she'd brought from Hand Me Ups.

"Thanks for letting me do this," she said.

"When we open for the season, you can stock some items for us to sell."

She smiled but made no promise.

Quickly, the volunteers got into place. All except for Kelly, who looked at Billy, a comical perplexed look on her face as she said, "It's just too cold for me to help with the hot chocolate and sweets outside. I think I'll work in the market."

"I could always use the help," Maggie agreed.

"That would make it too crowded." Kelly looked thoughtful for a moment, before saying, "Billy, bring me the quilted bag I left by the door."

In a moment Billy was back and Kelly was unloading the Santa outfit she'd been furtively working on for the last few days. She fluffed it out.

Jared saw Maggie's eyebrows raise. "Not Santa!" she breathed.

"Mrs. Claus!" the kids yelled.

Jared watched Maggie back up as the outfit was handed from kid to kid until it made its way to her. She held it up. A long-sleeved red dress with white marabou trim was just her size. It looked like it would fall to right above her knees. Kelly handed over a package of new red tights. "Here's the hat, too."

"I can't be Mrs. Claus. I have a shop to run."

"I've done fine all week without you. You help Jared."

"Please, Mom."

"Mom? I like that. Oh, and here's one more thing, an early Christmas present for you to unwrap."

Maggie shot Kelly a look that made Jared glad he had nothing to do with this plan.

Where Kelly got the package, Jared didn't see. Maggie quickly opened it and pulled out…red cowboy boots.

"They were Cassidy's idea," Kelly said. "I added the white fur. You can take it off later."

"You do know," Jared said, "Mrs. Claus always sits on Mr. Claus's lap for the first picture."

The look in Maggie's eyes told him that he'd better stay out of kicking range of her boots.

Mike Russell didn't even suggest that Maggie climb on Jared's lap. He just grinned and said, "The Lord works in mysterious ways."

"More like my mother-in-law works in mysterious ways," Maggie muttered.

From six-thirty on, there was a continuous line. The McClanahans and Jared's boys were elves leading people through the maze. Beth was the helper who organized the line. Maggie led children to Santa and arranged them for their picture.

First, though, Santa always asked what they wanted for Christmas.

For the most part, the requests were the same. "I want a new video game."

"I want a doll."

"I want a skateboard."

"I want a horse."

At least Cassidy wasn't the only one.

One little boy broke Maggie's heart. "I want my granddaddy to go away," he whispered in Santa's ear. "I prayed about it. Can you take him to the North Pole? He likes toys." Only Maggie and Mike Russell were close enough to hear.

Mike took over. "Why is that?"

"He makes my mommy cry."

Jared's eyes met Maggie's over the little boy's head. Mike gave a quick shake of his head.

"Can I put something under the tree for you?" Jared, er, Santa, asked.

"A puzzle. Granddaddy will help me put it together."

A few minutes later, there was finally a lull and Maggie said to Mike, "Did you know that little boy?"

"That was Joshua Phillips. Hillary's youngest son."

Maggie remembered what Jared had said, about Hillary's hard beginnings, who she was today, and parents who didn't deserve to be parents.

"Can we contact someone?" Maggie asked. "Social services or something?"

"Abe Phillips is just a strange old man," Mike said. "He makes Hillary cry because she's the sole breadwinner. He's never worked a day in his life. But, it's his house she lives in, and he watches the boys while she works. He does play with them. He's the kind of guy who never grew up. They wouldn't be better off, at least right now, without him."

"That's sad."

"It is, but if you knew the situation five years ago, you'd know how much better it is now and how much hope both Hillary and her dad have."

"But," Maggie said, "that little boy is praying that his grandpa goes away. That can't be good."

"Have you ever heard of First Chronicles 28:9?"

Maggie shook her head. Thanks to her short marriage to Dan, she knew the stories of the Bible, the lessons therein, but she'd not had the opportunity or teachings to put many verses to memory.

"For the Lord searches every heart and understands every motive behind the thoughts."

Maggie let out a breath, loud enough for Jared to hear. He looked at her. Tears, quickly stopped by the cold, brimmed just beyond her cheeks. "Oh, oh."

"Maggie, are you okay?"

"Is that scripture for real?"

"Yes, and it's one of my favorites," Mike said. "If God answered some of the prayers I've uttered in haste, I'd be in trouble."

"Ohhhh." Maggie felt her body relax, like something escaping—guilt?—to let something else take its place—joy?

An elf came through the maze right in front of more kids. Maggie wiped her eyes and got back to business. This time, there was a lightness to her step and the joy of the season followed her every movement. Between children, she looked at Jared.

He looked back and she nodded yes to the questions in his eyes.

Then, suddenly, it was her own daughter's turn on Santa's lap.

Cassidy didn't seem to remember that Santa was really Jared. She crawled up on his lap, not needing Maggie's assistance, and reached into her pocket.

"I brought my list."

"Let me see it."

Maggie peered over Jared's shoulder and read aloud, "Red cowboy boots, puppy, baby brother, horse and a daddy."

"Hmm." Jared looked at Maggie and said, "I think I can help with most of those. Do you want me to…?"

Mike Russell just barely got the camera ready in time to photograph the kiss Maggie Tate gave Jared as she joined her daughter on Santa's lap and said, "I do."

Epilogue

"It's perfect," Maggie said.

Beth looked in the mirror, first front and then back before finally going sideways just to do it all again.

Maggie smiled. Everything about the light, ivory-colored organza-over-satin dress suited the artistic Beth, from the embroidered tulips, looking three dimensional, to the attached double sash that attached to the train also embroidered with tulips. The nipped waistline to the princess-seamed bust molded perfectly to Beth's body.

"Mrs. Tate, can I really wear it?"

"Call me Kelly and absolutely. That's why I had it sent. I knew when I saw the McCreedy's living room and realized the Christmas theme for your wedding, that my old wedding dress was perfect."

Beth looked at Maggie. "And you don't mind that I'm not wearing the one you've been repairing?"

"Oh," Maggie said slowly, "I think somebody else might get to wear that dress." Walking over, she took it down and admired it.

"Try it on," Beth urged.

"She has," Kelly said. "Twice that I'm aware of."

"Just to make sure the alterations were smooth."

Beth and Kelly exchanged a look that clearly communicated "Yeah, right."

"I'll just put on the lace overcoat so you can see how it looks now that I've repaired it."

Gently, Maggie took it from the soft hanger. It fell to her shoulders perfectly. The sleeves tapered at her wrists.

"Wow," Beth said.

Kelly nodded.

Downstairs, the bell above the door sounded and kids' voices filled the shop. Cassidy and Caleb's volume were always on high.

"Well," came a shout, "did you find the perfect dress?"

"Joel, don't come up!" Beth shouted.

"Can I come up?" Jared's voice, deep and rich, questioned.

"You can't come up, either!" Beth shouted. "You can't see the bride." Quietly, she added, "And I'm not talking about me."

Maggie took off the overcoat and returned it to the hanger.

"I'll step down and see how the men are doing."

Beth chuckled. "Men, right. You mean the *man.*"

"I guess I do." Maggie opened the door to her shop and took a few steps down, only to meet Jared who was already more than halfway up. As he caught her to him in a tight embrace, she shouted up to Beth, "Oh, and I like spats, too. I've already told Jared to consider wearing them at your wedding as practice."

"So he's wearing them?" Beth sounded excited.

"You should see how quickly I put them on," Jared answered right before he bent down to kiss his future wife.

* * * * *

Dear Reader,

If only children come with how-to booklets!

My husband and I are blessed with an active son who constantly amazes us. As we travel the road called parenthood, I'm grateful to have a helpmate to brainstorm, encourage and, yes, rein me in occasionally.

Maggie Tate values control and dependability—laced with love. She's a constant in her daughter's life. Her flaw is thinking "I know best."

I'm often guilty of this flaw myself.

Jared, on the other hand, is a single dad well aware of his shortcomings. He's ready to settle down again. He's looking for someone exactly like his late wife, his childhood sweetheart.

Both Maggie and Jared think they know best. But, really, God knows best.

Thank you for reading *Once Upon a Christmas*. It's my first Christmas story. I had so much fun writing it. Please visit me at my website www.pamelatracy.com.

Pamela Tracy

Questions for Discussion

1. When the story opens both Jared and Maggie are sitting in the principal's office with their offspring. Have you been in this position? What goes through your head? Do you blame yourself? Others? What should the consequences be for "throwing a lunch box"?

2. For the beginning of the story, there's concern that Caleb might have difficulty with focus. How did Jared react? Do men react differently than women when faced with such situations? Why did he realize he needed to talk with Maggie? What did she offer that he couldn't have found himself?

3. Maggie's distrustful at first. She thinks Jared had good intentions but she's not sure he'll follow through. What makes her feel this way? Does Jared live up to expectations or does he surprise her? What did he do especially well in dealing with Caleb? What did she notice?

4. Maggie no longer attends church. She has reasons. If you were her best friend, and knew these reasons, what would you say to her? Make a list of five things. Then, compare your list with others around you who have also made lists. Rank them in order of importance.

5. Jared surprises himself by asking Maggie to go pick out Christmas trees. What motivated his change of heart? Was it seeing the photos and realizing what he was missing from his and his children's life? Was it the thought that she'd lost her husband last Christmas and he felt empathy? Or, at this time, deep down was he already seeing Maggie as more than just a mother to ask advice of?

6. Describe the visit to the Totwells from Maggie's point of view. What did she see and think? Describe the visit from Jared's point of view. What did he see and think? Were there any indicators that Kyle was the thief? At the end of the story, what do you think will happen to their farm? What will happen to them?

7. Billy admits that he made a mistake by not asking Joel permission to marry his mother. What was he trying to point out to Jared? What function does each of Jared's boys have in the story? How will adding Maggie and Cassidy to the family change their roles?

8. When Kelly Tate shows up, Maggie's opinion of her changes. Quite quickly. What helps Kelly ease herself into Maggie's life? What helps Maggie be accepting of her mother-in-law's role? What do both want?

9. As we near the end of *Once Upon a Christmas,* we find that some of the money collected in the Christmas maze will go to the Totwell family. How did this idea come about? What in the Bible encourages such an endeavor? Some of the people who lost presents were not Christians. What does this show them?

10. At the end, Maggie hears the scripture "For the Lord searches every heart and understands every motive behind the thoughts." What does this tell her about her prayer? What does it feel like when guilt releases its hold? How do we keep the joy when we realize God's true power? How do you think Jared reacted when she told him what had kept her from church so long?

REQUEST YOUR FREE BOOKS!

2 FREE INSPIRATIONAL NOVELS
PLUS 2
FREE
MYSTERY GIFTS

Love Inspired

YES! Please send me 2 FREE Love Inspired® novels and my 2 FREE mystery gifts (gifts are worth about $10). After receiving them, if I don't wish to receive any more books, I can return the shipping statement marked "cancel." If I don't cancel, I will receive 6 brand-new novels every month and be billed just $4.49 per book in the U.S. or $4.99 per book in Canada. That's a saving of at least 22% off the cover price. It's quite a bargain! Shipping and handling is just 50¢ per book in the U.S. and 75¢ per book in Canada.* I understand that accepting the 2 free books and gifts places me under no obligation to buy anything. I can always return a shipment and cancel at any time. Even if I never buy another book, the two free books and gifts are mine to keep forever.

105/305 IDN FEGR

Name	(PLEASE PRINT)	

Address		Apt. #

City	State/Prov.	Zip/Postal Code

Signature (if under 18, a parent or guardian must sign)

Mail to the **Reader Service:**
IN U.S.A.: P.O. Box 1867, Buffalo, NY 14240-1867
IN CANADA: P.O. Box 609, Fort Erie, Ontario L2A 5X3

Not valid for current subscribers to Love Inspired books.

**Are you a subscriber to Love Inspired books
and want to receive the larger-print edition?
Call 1-800-873-8635 or visit www.ReaderService.com.**

* Terms and prices subject to change without notice. Prices do not include applicable taxes. Sales tax applicable in N.Y. Canadian residents will be charged applicable taxes. Offer not valid in Quebec. This offer is limited to one order per household. All orders subject to credit approval. Credit or debit balances in a customer's account(s) may be offset by any other outstanding balance owed by or to the customer. Please allow 4 to 6 weeks for delivery. Offer available while quantities last.

Your Privacy—The Reader Service is committed to protecting your privacy. Our Privacy Policy is available online at www.ReaderService.com or upon request from the Reader Service.

We make a portion of our mailing list available to reputable third parties that offer products we believe may interest you. If you prefer that we not exchange your name with third parties, or if you wish to clarify or modify your communication preferences, please visit us at www.ReaderService.com/consumerchoice or write to us at Reader Service Preference Service, P.O. Box 9062, Buffalo, NY 14269. Include your complete name and address.

LIREG11B